DESIGN FOR LIFE

DESIGN FOR LIFE

Essie Summers

Thorndike Press • Chivers Press
Thorndike, Maine USA   Bath, England

This Large Print edition is published by Thorndike Press, USA and by Chivers Press, England.

Published in 1998 in the U.S. by arrangement with Chivers Press Ltd.

Published in 1998 in the U.K. by arrangement with Severn House Publishers.

U.S. Hardcover   0-7862-1048-6   (Romance Series Edition)
U.K. Hardcover   0-7540-1095-3   (Windsor Large Print)
U.K. Softcover   0-7540-2067-3   (Paragon Large Print)

The text of this Large Print edition is unabridged.
Other aspects of the book may vary from the original edition.

Set in 16 pt. Plantin by Rick Gundberg.

Printed in the United States on permanent paper.

British Library Cataloguing in Publication Data available

Library of Congress Cataloging in Publication Data

Summers, Essie.
    Design for life / Essie Summers.
      p.   cm.
    ISBN 0-7862-1048-6 (lg. print : hc : alk. paper)
    1. Large type books. I. Title.
[PR9639.3.S89D47   1998]
823—dc21   97-31641

To the memory of Miss Robertson, whose given name I never knew, of Christchurch Technical College in the Long-ago.

Tribute to Shakespeare

I have loved Shakespeare almost all my days
  Since first a well-loved teacher brought to
    me
The sheer enchantment of his singing ways
  With word and wit and mirth and tragedy;
Have stood beside him as his jocund day
  Stood tiptoe on his mountains when the
    light
Of night's poor candles paled beneath the
  ray
  Of rising sun; have tasted the delight
Of moonlight sleeping sweetly on the bank;
  Known the sweet scent distilled from
    Shakespeare's rose;
Heard clash of ancient warfare, rank on
  rank;

Felt Shakespeare's gentle peace at long
   day's close.
I had loved England long before the time
   I first beheld her in her silvered sea,
As in this southern world, this far-flung
   clime,
   I at my schoolroom desk read avidly
Of that far country, demi-paradise,
   That other Eden and I knew that I
Would someday shape my words to pay the
   price
   To cross the seas to see his English sky.
. . . When that day came, my spirit knelt
   in awe
   To meet at last fulfilment of a dream,
I trod where he had trod so long before
   And, like my Shakespeare, mused by
      Avon's stream.
I offer thanks for every matchless word
   Composed by reeking rushlight as he
      sought
To pin on page the brook, the rose, the bird,
   For those to come, in written rapture
      caught.
This then is what puts all our doubts at rest,
   He is not dead, he cannot ever be
The while his deathless lines show forth the
   best
   Of life and love, True Immortality.

The author wishes to record her thanks to
Jacqueline Brash, without whose practical
help this book might never have been
produced.
And also for the bonus of realising, many
years later, that she, like me, grew up
knowing every inch of the
Port Hills and Harbour.

Chapter One

Dane Inglethorpe sank into a deep chair at Victoria and Blair Doig's Haslemere home and said, "Now I can unpin this fixed smile and really relax. Signing books was once a novelty and an honour but I've reached saturation point. This tour from Glasgow back to London is a bit too near my return to New Zealand. It's been a wonderful experience and I've met some great people in all walks of life, who've had relaxation from my thrillers, and from now on I'll feel I'm writing for real folk not just faceless readers, and I'll be inspired, I know, but at the moment I've got personality indigestion! I'd like to rusticate with you and Blair around this magnificent estate he manages."

Victoria decided that right now wasn't the time to mention that a request from his publisher was coming his way. She'd never heard this broad-shouldered, vital, Kiwi male admit to exhaustion before . . . a very rugged farmer-cum-author.

She poured the tea, uncovered sandwiches and pikelets and saw him begin to relax.

"No doubt everyone back home will be envying you the sort of high life you've had to indulge in these past few months and will never guess burgeoning fame can also be mighty hard work."

He put two sandwiches together and bit into them, and then said with relish: "Oh . . . cold mutton . . . that takes me back to my own paddocks and the sound of bleating on the hills above the bay." He grinned, "I feel I'm a victim of split personality — one part of my mind asking can this possibly be me? The other terribly nostalgic for the sweep of the Peninsula Hills and the salt tang of the harbour . . . the boats rocking at our jetty and the sight of ships coming in to port at Lyttelton just opposite."

Victoria nodded. "I can understand that, though when I came here I had the compensation of being with Blair at last, all misunderstandings resolved, but I did know homesickness, though our trips back helped and Surrey is so beautiful. When you've shaken off this surfeit of signing and interviews, Dane, you'll get a thrill again of knowing your next book is to be serialised for TV, making it possible for you to restore your lovely inlet to the place it deserves in New Zealand colonial history. It will make Hauroko Bay viable again in these days of narrowing world markets, tariffs and tough competition, and make it possible for your sister and her husband to carry on, especially with her idea of restoring the other homestead into a tourist attraction. With her experience it could make all the difference to Phyl and Ross."

He chuckled. "I feel better already, Victoria. With your own wide experience of interior decorating, I can begin to believe that the residue of that replica village that's been a millstone round the necks of every generation since old Aubrey Inglethorpe chucked it in and went back to England, leaving the bay to the seagulls and the rabbits, may give Phyl and Ross a more profitable life. It was different for me. I suppose I could write anywhere."

She looked at him shrewdly. "Though it would tear the heart out of you to give up farming altogether, wouldn't it?"

He nodded. "Thanks, Victoria. That about sums it up. I've got to look on this latest success as a godsend . . . saving the place I love best on earth, for future generations. Till now of course we've managed to keep the exteriors sound — though I felt the effort shortened Dad's life — and if it can be made to pay its way, I might, in time, be able to buy back the land Dad sold to provide the upkeep. Since I've been here and seen how some of these estates have managed to have been retained in the family despite the crippling death duties they suffered, I think that dream is within our grasp."

Victoria refilled his cup. "You know, Dane, something like this happened to me in my working life back home. I still feel a sense of achievement about it, though it was quite a long time ago. The firm I worked for sometimes sent me off as a consultant to wealthy sheepstation owners to restore pioneer homesteads and to look for antiques for the firm as I went. You probably wouldn't remember, as you were just a youngster when you used to holiday at my parents' place in Central Otago. This old home was going on the market and it was breaking the hearts of three elderly sisters to leave it. I persuaded them to turn it into a tourist attraction — my firm got the contract and I planned the decorating and it did well. A nephew and his wife run it now. I'd love to think that your deserted village, that's been such a white elephant for so long, could prove an asset. If I wasn't so tied up with the children's educational needs I'd come out myself to do it up for you — or at least supervise."

Dane laughed. "I can imagine Blair's reaction — he'd dump me in the horse trough. But it does need an expert. Any chance of your old firm back home being interested?" She shook her head. "They're just in the antique business now. I wish I could magic up someone like I did for Rupert Airlie of The Lake of the Kingfisher — I sent Elissa Montgomery out. Her mother had been the governess there long before. Elissa thought Rupert must have been thinking of re-marrying — he later sought her mother out in Canada and wed her, and Elissa married the head shepherd."

"Well — put the great brain to work and find someone for me, though my sister is married to *my* head shepherd. Oh, I know we have some good restorers in New Zealand but since I've seen some of the restored houses here — the smaller village ones I mean — I feel that's what's needed to realise old Aubrey's dream. It was patterned so much more on the English style."

Victoria felt she mustn't postpone any longer the message from his publisher. "Dane, you're going to get a call soon from London; Mr Burford has a proposition. I'm afraid it's a final signing session in a village not far from here." At that moment the phone rang. It was for Dane. She said, "Yes,

13

he's here. I'm afraid I haven't had a chance to explain. He was rather bushed when he arrived, but is probably up to it now."

Dane mouthed 'Traitor!' at her and took the phone. Miles Burford confirmed his worst fears even though he was a great guy and Dane owed him so much for his success. He said, "I'm afraid this is an opportunity not to be missed. Rather different from the usual, not a bookshop at all — an antique shop at a place near you called Seddon Halt. The owner is a most remarkable woman, known far and wide as Leonora. People travel great distances to see her wares. She's shrewd and rather choosy, so this is a great compliment to you.

"She's become a great fan of your books and is willing — indeed keen — to make a display of all your titles and have you there. Seems she doesn't sell New Zealand mementoes but has a private collection of them that came into her possession years ago and after reading your books has got all fired up with this idea. I went down to see her, though I knew the place — we bought some choice stuff from her some time ago. She has a first-class window dresser, her granddaughter I believe, who has designed some excellent murals based on the book jacket of the one you wrote using your own bay as the setting — or rather Lyttelton Harbour. It'll be well advertised — we'll pick up the tab for that — and, anticipating your agreement, will send down a van load of three titles. What did you say, Dane?"

"I didn't say anything, I just groaned!" he muttered.

Victoria looked horrified. The publisher's every word had been clear to her. Then she was relieved to hear Dane chuckle and say, "It's okay. I realise you had to fall in with the idea. I'll go across this morning if it's as near as that, and arrange for a session fairly soon — I've still some sightseeing to do before leaving. I want some notes about Hampshire for a book I have in mind. What?" He listened and checked another groan, then said, "Yes, I expect you had to agree about that. I'll do three sessions. Yes, I realise they gather momentum. Anybody will tell you, Miles, you can talk anyone into anything. Will do. Wish you well for your business in Hamburg and I'll report to you when I get back."

He put the phone down and spread his hands out in a despairing gesture. "And I was so looking forward to you showing me some of the villages round here. But I'd better go over right away and get the first approach over. Good thing I came early. I

15

only hope I like these murals the grand-daughter has done or I'll offend the formidable Leonora."

Victoria shook her head. "You won't. She isn't formidable — just a very shrewd businesswoman. And the murals will be good — that girl belonged to our firm and has done them for very high-class tasks we were taking on. She got a long leave of absence while Leonora spent some weeks in Canada with some of her family, and managed the business very creditably I've heard. Don't get any unjustified preconceived ideas."

He laughed and heaved himself out of the comfortable chair. "Well, just tell me how to get there. I'll find somewhere there for lunch. Tell Blair I'll see him tonight."

The countryside was lovely. It had been a wonderful summer. Now, very shortly, he'd be heading into the southern hemisphere spring. How he'd love to take to some of these side roads leading into glorious woods where in spring he had seen carpets of bluebells beneath beeches that had met overhead as he and Blair had gone to Portsmouth and the Isle of Wight. Then he had taken copious notes for future books; now all he wanted to do was wander those leafy byways with no thought of the commercial side of authorship. Today, in any case, his mind was busy with the pros and cons of the project for Hauroko Bay. They'd lose a lot of privacy, of course. He'd have to make sure his writing hours weren't invaded. But Phyl must get her chance. He'd contact a Christchurch firm of interior decorators as soon as he returned. That ridiculous row of village houses would have to wait till they saw how the restaurant idea took on. In that area, Phyl was an expert. And now, blast it, three signing sessions lay ahead. He must find the high street. No doubt Leonora's would be easily recognisable . . . quaint, with a bow window displaying antique glass and porcelain and rarities, not at all the sort of premises to make an eye-catching display of an up-and-coming author's books.

He parked the car, strode on, saw an ancient small-paned window and then came to a halt. There were two bow windows but between them as modern and large an expanse of display windows as he'd seen. He guessed the antique windows had belonged to two separate houses and the other had been built to bridge the gap.

What he saw in the middle section brought him to a standstill. Here was a collection of Maori artefacts that would have

17

done credit to any museum, startling in authenticity, but it was the backdrop to the display that made him catch his breath. The murals curved round the beautifully grouped collection but they instantly transported him to his own bay — the hills, the houses, a glimpse of the tiny chapel, the blacksmith's shop that was still in use, the old stables with the ancient clock tower, a glimpse of an old-fashioned haystack; that surely must have been imagination on the part of the artist, the granddaughter Victoria had spoken of. The other details were faithful to the book cover. The side wings were devoted to other pioneer events associated with Lyttelton Harbour, a very good sketch of the First Four Ships that had anchored after long voyaging within days of each other in the summer of 1850; one of the small settlement of the port, with immigration quarters for the first brave settlers; a glimpse of the bridle path leading up over the hills to the plains of Canterbury and the capital-to-be of the new province. By jove, this girl had done her homework — there was even a picture of Captain Scott and a rough sketch of the ship in which he had sailed, early in the century, to his ill-fated expedition to the South Pole. They must have obtained these details from New Zealand

18

House. His animosity and reluctance fell away from him. He went in.

There were two or three assistants and someone who couldn't be anyone else but Leonora, busy with a customer. She was tall, with whitening hair showing traces of copper colour, very elegantly garbed. She was just finishing, wrapped the purchase herself, bade the man goodbye. Dane stepped nearer and said, "Leonora, I believe — I'm Dane Inglethorpe. Just got back to Haslemere this morning, and Miles Burford rang me."

What a handsome face this woman had — lined with experience, but her blue eyes sparkling with vitality. She was exquisitely made up. Her delight was genuine. She turned to an assistant, saying, "I'm not to be disturbed unless absolutely necessary," and led the way into her office. He found himself responding with a warmth he'd not expected to feel.

"I couldn't be more impressed. This is so spot on — for a moment I could imagine myself back home. You must have had access to an amazing source of very localised material, apart from the book jacket. May I ask how you came by all this?"

She laughed. "You couldn't be more surprised than I was when my granddaughter, reading this latest of yours exclaimed, 'Why Gran, here's a thriller about all those pictures and mementoes of those things you've got stored in your New Zealand room.' " She laughed again and continued. "I must admit that till then I hadn't read any of your books — perhaps naturally I stick to period novels — but I became so interested, at first because of this strange link, then so enamoured I read every paperback of yours Chloe possessed. Then this idea was born."

"Have you other South Pacific artefacts for selling to collectors?" he asked.

She shook her head. "No, I kept these for sentimental reasons. They didn't belong to my family even, but to a childless couple who were neighbours of my parents and were very good to a rather lonely little girl who was an only child. So they left them to me. She was quite an artist and had had some connection with New Zealand in her early years. She did mostly seascapes — there are some fine ones of the seas around Kaikoura and Wellington too. She didn't marry till fairly late in life."

He said: "I'd like to meet your granddaughter. She must be quite an artist herself."

"She is. Her work as an interior decorator has enhanced her gift. She's been quite in demand for murals to advertise several openings for new ventures. But I'm afraid she's out just now. It's her lunch hour. Will you come back? Sorry I can't take you to lunch myself but from twelve till two only half the staff is on duty. But there is a reasonably good restaurant about five doors up the street."

"Thanks — I can come back in say an hour. Would that be okay? Oh — Miles said that as soon as he knew I would take this on, he'd send down a load of books. I like the way you've stimulated public interest by having just that small easel in the centre with that placard saying 'Watch this space'."

He went out, pleasantly aware his interest was quickened. It was inspiring to find such localised publicity here from thirteen thousand miles away and, judging by Leonora's age, if these had belonged to her parents' neighbour, they were well and truly old.

The restaurant was rather crowded but a small table was found for him in a secluded corner at the far end. A wall topped with ferns and pot plants separated it from another small alcove. God bless Miles after all. The 'reasonably good' restaurant proved just that: an excellent soup, fish garnished with a delectable sauce, perfectly cooked vegetables. He was waiting for dessert when he became aware of a feminine voice behind him. It was a charming voice in timbre, sharpened a little with indignation. It said: "I can't believe this . . . you're actually proposing to me in a restaurant *and in my lunch hour!* How prosaic can a man get? I've heard it said that the age of chivalry is dead but it seems as if romance is too!"

Dane thought, Thank heaven I'm hidden by all this greenery, then, a secret gratification taking possession of him, But for sure this is grist to any author's mill. I'm getting at first hand, a modern girl's reaction to a twit of a modern male. Good for her!

He listened eagerly for the response. It was decidedly aggrieved. The silly fool! "Good grief — you don't really go for that sort of stuff do you? I mean love at first sight, moonlight and roses and so on. I thought we were both mature people and the time had come to put it to you."

It sounded as if the girl had thumped the table. "You must be mad! I don't think we've got a thing in common. In fact I know we haven't. No, I wasn't looking for love at first sight — I don't particularly believe in it — but there's got to be *something* to hold two people together, something that could mean moments of magic through whatever life demanded of them. Something *my* parents have so that even now they hate to be parted even for a week. You must have no imagination, no intuition. We have nothing in common, we'd never reach the heights together. I think that if you're ever going to marry anyone you'd better revolutionise your thinking. Great scott, I was reading a book last night that expressed just that and it was spoken by a man at that. He was talking of an impending marriage he thought was being entered into like a business proposition and he said: 'Doesn't love come with a sound of trumpets any more, like a song on the wind?' For goodness' sake Hudson, if everyone felt like you we'd never have had any immortal songs, any great operas, no sonnets from Shakespeare. Oh, you make me mad. I gave you no excuse whatever for thinking I'd marry you. Ours has been purely a business association, a few dinners, a couple of theatre trips. Look, I'm not waiting for dessert — it would choke me! It's me for a good brisk walk round the river bank. So goodbye!"

Dane couldn't resist a furtive glance as, following the scrape of a chair, a tall girl in a visible temper flashed by. He had a glimpse of coppery hair caught back at the nape of her neck, an angry chin out-thrust a little, and the whirlwind departed.

A waitress appeared with two colourful concoctions on a tray and Dane unashamedly listened as a voice, striving not to show chagrin, he thought, said: "My tablemate has suddenly remembered a business appointment she must keep and has had to rush away."

The waitress smiled. "Oh that's all right sir, we can all forget at times. But here's yours. Will you be wanting coffee?"

Dane heard the answer he expected. "Yes please, black and strong."

He permitted himself a sigh of satisfaction. The smug idiot. Glad he got his comeuppance. If all men conducted their proposals like that, what would poor bedevilled authors write about? Perhaps Miles had something when he advised him once to pep up the love interest.

His own dessert arrived so promptly he was almost sure it was the one the redheaded one had spurned. It was very good.

It was too early to go back to Leonora's yet. What a marvellous exit line that had been. He must get it down while he remembered the whole bit of dialogue. One phrase described his own bay perfectly . . . *hau* equalled wind, *roko* was the South Island form of *rongo* which meant sound . . . sounds borne upon the wind. He got out his notebook and began to write. A great scene for his next book. There had to be passionate encounters sandwiched in among the danger zones of thriller writing. He took it down almost word for word as he recalled it, added an idea of his own in the form of the dialogue being heard by a hero-type who resolves to present the girl with evidence of romantic love! At the end he wrote 'Good for you coppertop, whoever you are!' then added, 'What a bit of luck for me.'

He had no idea of the havoc those notes would make of *his* life.

Leonora came to meet him. "I hope you had an excellent lunch." He assured her it had exceeded his expectations and grinned to himself. She added, "My granddaughter should have been back by now. Oh, here she is." Dane turned towards the door and there coming through was the furious red-head!

The bright hair was loosened a little as if it had been braced against the breeze off the river, and her colour was high. But otherwise, no one could have guessed she'd recently been the centre of a splendid row. He gave her full marks for the way she greeted him. No hint of disturbance in the way she lifted her eyes, eyes that quickened with interest as Leonora made the introduction. The eyes were a clear translucent green and to his immense surprise he found himself saying: "Why, your eyes are exactly the colour of the waters of Lyttelton Harbour!"

It checked the words on her lips and the next moment he was contrite. "Oh, do excuse me, I don't know what came over me to be so personal."

She took it easily, said, "Oh well we don't expect authors to be like other lesser mortals. Think nothing of it."

He grinned. "I used to be just an ordinary run-of-the-mill farmer. Suddenly acquiring fame must have gone to my head."

The grandmother had a twinkle in her eye. She finished the introductions with, "Chloe Lambard is my son's girl. She managed my business very well during a three months' break I took in Canada recently."

Chloe looked up at him, "So your name really is Dane Inglethorpe! I thought it sounded like a pen name and you'd turn out to be James Brown or William Smith. I'm so glad it's really your name." Then she clapped her hands to her mouth. "What am I saying?"

He laughed. "It must be catching, speaking thoughts aloud, but at least with me you could put it down to being a reincarnation of the original 'Wild Colonial Boy'."

"But I've no excuse. I've been trained by Gran to meet the elite, and by my firm of decorators in correct behaviour towards their clients, many of them titled."

He said firmly, "Just make it Dane. Even the rouseabouts in our shearing shed make it that. We're a casual lot. And may I make it Chloe? I like it as a name."

"Yes of course — it's a thrill to meet you. I've read all your books. Not like Gran who just got interested when she recognised the setting of this book but then became fascinated and has since read all you've written. It's good to meet you. I find someone with an imagination like yours rather refreshing after some of our tame business contacts of late."

He thought to himself, Yes, *very* lately — but you've no idea *I* know.

He uttered aloud: "I've got a fellow feeling. I came back to Victoria and Blair feeling very jaded. Too many signing sessions all much the same. But this is refreshingly different. All I could think of after the last one was how glad I'd be to get back to our farm."

Chloe said, "Our?", then thought how inquisitive — she *was* speaking out of turn today. Naturally you'd expect this man in

27

his thirties to have a wife.

He explained. "My sister and I share the property. That's as it should be; after experience in hotel management over here she came back to marry my head shepherd — a sterling fellow. Now she wants to turn the homestead into a tourist venture. It will help us preserve our old village, that is such a liability. You'll know how I described it in my book. Fine as a setting for a thriller, but a millstone in upkeep."

"How did it come about? Sounds quaint for New Zealand. I thought that when Gran first showed me an old sketch of the bay. Then, of course, she recognised it on the book jacket."

"There is one other one in Mid-Canterbury," he told her, "between the distant coastline of the plains and the Southern Alps, called Barrhill. Goes back, the same as ours, to pioneer settlers with grandiose ideas. Like old Aubrey Inglethorpe, though he wasn't old then, of course; he too finally returned to England. My forebear, though we're not in direct descent, sent 'Home' for people from his own village and built a replica one in the bay. He gave them great opportunities; occasionally I come across descendants of them mainly over the hills to Canterbury, but one or two still live around the harbour hills. The idea of owning their own farms proved more alluring than staying in the same bay under the thumb of Aubrey. He'd set up a wool-scouring plant and did well for long enough but the depression of the 1880s hit him badly and this miniature village street was deserted. But the oaks and beeches and walnuts still survive — magnificent specimens. All English trees do well in New Zealand and we've the lovely evergreen native bush in every gully too."

The sea-green eyes sparkled. "I so enjoyed reading of an authentic setting. Is it exactly as you described it?"

"Except for the secret tunnels I used for the purpose of the story — the skulduggery bits — yes."

She said: "The idea of a deserted village was romance in itself. It caught my fancy and recalled Goldsmith's poem on one . . . 'Sweet Auburn, loveliest village of the plain, Where peace and plenty cheered the labouring swain, Where smiling spring her earliest visit paid, and long-departing summer still delayed'." His voice had joined hers in the last line.

"By the time I get home, smiling spring will be paying her first visit and I'll get this scheme under way. In the earlier days this

29

property didn't have the happiest history, but it's had it since, with our childhood and now with Phyl and Ross's children. So we forget those two sadder times."

Chloe felt she detected a rueful note. "And presumably your children, in time."

He nodded. "I'd like to think so, can't think of a lovelier place to grow up in . . . the hills, the harbour, the open sea beyond, the gulls crying and the larks high in the sky. But unless we make a success of this venture of Phyl's it's not viable in size now to support two families. Only my books have made it possible. It's a dream come true for my sister and her husband."

Chloe could imagine that. "Perhaps it's lovelier than Goldsmith's village of the plain, with the sea at its door. Tell me is it really that colour? These sketches Gran came by don't show the colour of course and they are shabby to boot, but your description made it sound so vivid and the book jacket accentuated that. To make sure of it I rang New Zealand House before attempting the murals. I felt someone might know, and the girl they put me on to became quite indignant and said indeed it was. I liked her indignation.

"She was from Christchurch and said the harbour had been created from volcanic action aeons ago and it was thought that accounted for it and that there were two extinct volcanoes; that over the hills behind your bay was Akaroa Harbour with a distinctly different colour, more like turquoise with the most unusual streaks in it, almost burgundy — except when storms lashed both and they became battleship grey. She was entitled to indignation. I felt the same way once when I was accused of seeing everything through rose-coloured glasses, though I felt sorry for the one who made the remark. I felt the person was spiritually colour blind, and how drab that life must be. Just as if sunsets and rainbows aren't as real as stormclouds and forbidding granite cliffs!"

"Bravo!" said Dane. "You were right to pity him. I'd never have got my first book accepted if I didn't use the beauty of my settings as a contrast to evil doings and ugly happenings." He thought it sounded like something the anaemic Hudson might say, so he was probably right to assume 'him'.

The girl laughed and swung her shoulder-bag off. "We'd better go into the office — mine, not Gran's. I've got it rather littered at the moment with paints and brushes. I got fired up with this — such a change from backdrops of Doulton and willow pattern."

31

She could be practical too, and got down right away to practical issues with times to suit him, yet with an eye to best shopping hours. She said anxiously, "I hope I portrayed the foreign ships okay, the sort that would slip in and out with contraband cargoes, drugs and so on."

"Indeed you did. That caught my eye too. I felt I must've done justice to those happenings for you to have been able to portray them so well. Do you ever design dust covers? You should."

She flushed with pleasure. How could she have ever dreamed it could come to this when she'd read and loved his first book? Leonora came in. They ratified the times, then Chloe asked, "What did you mean, Dane, when you said that, twice, the history of the bay had been a sad one?"

He explained. "It had passed to a nephew who also came from England. Later he went back and married his boyhood sweetheart and brought her here. He expected her to love it as he did but she couldn't settle, found the life too remote, as it was in those days. She had been reared in an atmosphere of parties and theatres, and Gregory Inglethorpe wasn't an articulate man, to make her feel loved and cherished. In the end she ran away; just couldn't face telling him. He was angry and bitter at first and didn't want her back, then someone from the harbour ran into her in a north country city street and saw she was obviously pregnant. This woman begged her to return but she wouldn't, said it wouldn't be right to return for that reason only. The woman told Gregory and he took passage to England immediately, was ready to sell up and settle back 'Home' with her. I believe it seemed as if that would be the happy ending, but three days after their reunion he died of an unsuspected heart flaw. It had the effect on the poor mother-to-be — shouldering such a load of guilt — that she wouldn't take a penny from the estate for her or for her child, and so when the executors of Gregory's will tried to trace her, she had completely disappeared. Her people had moved away with her." He looked across the table they were working at and was surprised to see tears in Leonora's eyes. He'd put her down as more of a tough businesswoman. He liked seeing those tears. "It then passed to another branch of the family — our branch — and the history has been a very happy one since."

"And will be happier soon, now you can maintain it as it should be," Chloe added. "My grandmother never ceases to amaze me

— I've read *all* your books, but she reads *one* and gets all fired up with ideas of having you in here signing books — then burns the midnight oil catching up on all your others." She gave her a comradely grin. "As long as she doesn't make a habit of it. She might land me with an author whose books I don't like. This project I found inspiring. Though of course when she realised your book jacket was familiar to her from her New Zealand collection, that jolted her into action."

"Yes, I found that interesting. How did you come by it, Mrs Lambard?"

"Make it Leonora. Everybody does. The memorabilia? That's easy. Not in my own fossickings. My parents had these close neighbours, I believe I mentioned them earlier. A childless couple older than Mother and Father. When they died I was left these things because I'd always been fascinated by them. I kept them as a showpiece when I married an antique dealer. Couldn't bear to sell them."

Chloe looked across at her grandmother and wondered a little that she hadn't disclosed how good those neighbours had been, adopting the small Leonora when both parents had lost their lives in a boating accident. But, of course, it would be a sad note to introduce.

Now and then Dane felt amazement sweep over him. At this time yesterday all he'd felt was thankfulness that all the signing was behind him, and unfettered freedom would be his for the remainder of his stay. He had been looking forward to the day he'd board the plane that was to take him to Singapore, Sydney, and home to Christchurch, set in that sea-girt isle. Now he felt invigorated, inspired. He must be mad.

He crossed to other evidences of Chloe's artistic ability . . . rough sketches of other settings and periods. No doubt part of her own work in decorating, but useful to Leonora too . . . canvases stacked in racks, all labelled 'Victorian', 'Queen Anne', 'Tudor', 'Carolinian', even 'Plantagenet' and 'Saxon'. She played down his congratulations. "Oh just part of my work and an interest in art inherited from Grandad."

"These make me realise how steeped in history you must be," Dane told her. "Our colonial history would seem raw to you, not quite two centuries old yet."

She considered it. "I don't know — when I was reading your book I found myself mentally restoring the derelict houses; inside I mean — you'd stressed they were well kept up outside. Suited the story. I felt it would be a challenge. Don't think my firm

restores only castles and manor houses —
I've had some of my greatest satisfaction
doing up old farmhouses and cottages."

It was then that Dane Inglethorpe felt that
the idea that had teased his mind talking to
Victoria, took on the dimensions of an ob-
session. Was there or wasn't there a chance,
if he proposed this idea, that she and her
grandmother might consider it? Probably
not. But he'd chance his luck.

Chapter Two

Chloe Lambard laughed. "When I was reading your book I found myself wondering if it really was as you described it, or if you'd portrayed it that way for the purposes of the story. But despite those doubts — which were natural seeing it was fiction not fact — I found myself mentally doing up those houses on the inside. You'd said they were well-kept, outwardly. Yet the breathless excitement of the intrigue and the chase held me."

The tawny eyes met the green ones across the table and held the look, a strange look for two people so recently met.

He said, rather quickly, "I'd better clarify something. The larger homestead Phyl and Ross want to improve is the second house on the property though very little older. Aubrey built a smaller one first but he and his wife both had ambitious ideas and the first one had not enough large rooms for the entertaining they did in those days — the upper classes anyway — dances at which the guests came long distances in horse-drawn vehicles . . . and there were no wall-flowers because women were scarce, so Inglethorpe House is basically suited for this venture."

"Oh I can just see it all," said Chloe. "I do hope they — you — as a family have many well-preserved photographs."

"We have. You mean they could be displayed?"

"I do. Nothing brings the past of a house more to life than representations of the people who formerly lived there . . . those who loved there, laughed there, mourned there, of course in our work these were massive portraits, but early colonial life sounds good to me."

"I moved into the older house when my sister got married. Not fair to a young couple otherwise — a three-cornered household — and these days, of course, a certain solitude is necessary for my writing. Some day I'll get round to restoring my house."

Leonora was called into one of the showrooms. Chloe was absorbed, her elbows on the table, her chin sunk in her hands, a good audience.

For a moment Dane lost the thread of his conversation as his mind switched back to the overheard clash at the restaurant. Fancy any guy proposing in a prosaic manner like that to this vital creature! She was responsive to all he'd told her of that young colony and its colourful life, to the dreams and ambitions, its desire to create something like the culture they had left behind . . . he thought afresh of all they had attempted: cutting a hazardous road around those formidable cliffs: driving a tunnel through to give access to Christchurch, to the easier life of the plains. A colossal task to contemplate, but crowned with the joyous surprise, for the contractors, of finding immense chambered caves beneath.

Chloe spoke. "I read up all the library could supply, the gallant way they sent men and horses to the Boer War and later more troops to the two world wars on the other side of the world." She stopped, said: "What are you looking at, Dane?"

"That," he said pointing. "That half-finished mural. It's Captain Scott and his *Terra Nova* — the ship of his last expedition setting sail from Lyttelton about 1910 or so."

"I got so interested in Gran's reaction to your book when she recognised Lyttelton was the original of the sketches in with the artefacts. Oh, there are a lot of other places too . . . a big sweep of bay over the hills, one or two identified on the back, but none of them signed, more's the pity. Was it Pegasus Bay?"

"Yes, it goes from Sumner, a lovely resort a few miles from Christchurch, and beyond it leagues of a surf shore, reaching to the Seaward Kaikouras, a mountain range. Fairly large rivers intersect, all well-bridged now."

"Yes, one of the pictures was of Kaikoura, a tiny seaside town. Don't they do whale-watching there now? I saw a TV feature on it. That was the only one named but others looked like that area. Perhaps the artist lived there. There were only a few of your bay and village. Must have taken the artist's fancy."

Leonora appeared, excusing herself for the long absence. "But it was quite profitable," she added; "and, by the way, there's a message for you Chloe, from Hudson. He'd like to take you for a moonlight drive. You're to ring him." A crease appeared between Leonora's brows, "A new line for him to take. It's usually some theatre, isn't it?"

Chloe didn't turn a hair. He admired her for that. "Then I'll get one of the staff to ring him. I don't want to break this up. It doesn't suit me Gran. It won't spoil any business dealings you have with him, will it? But I think I'll invent a prior engagement."

Dane said swiftly, "If I put something to you right now, including Leonora, could you look on that as 'prior'? It had been running through my mind as we talked."

Chloe's lips twitched. "How very opportune. But only if you can spare the time."

He said smoothly, "We need to discuss the signing sessions in more detail. I'll take you both to dinner. Victoria Doig should be able to suggest where."

There were no hesitations — perhaps Leonora preferred to keep an eye on Chloe's escorts! Chloe contented herself by saying, "You'll think I'm as impulsive as my grandmama — but not quite. We call her the human dynamo in the family circle. The only thing is, we mustn't encroach on what time you have left here."

He grinned, "Well if this is encroachment I'm all for it. Encroach on; I find it inspiring, to meet up with people so knowledgeable about my particular corner of the globe. A signing session with a difference. What if I pick you up at seven-thirty?"

He felt an admiration for this coppertop. She wasn't worrying about the unimaginative Hudson. A spirited filly who knew her own mind. So too, it seemed, did Leonora.

Also he admitted to himself, an intriguing situation for an author to brood upon. Good copy. An unimaginative lover . . . then enter the hero!

The dinner, the conversation and the setting proved convivial. Dane's exhaustion had disappeared. It wasn't till they were at the coffee stage that Chloe was startled to hear Dane say: "Maybe I move as fast as Leonora but time may be the essence of this. Victoria told me of someone from your firm, some years back, going out to New Zealand to one of our lake country estates to do a job in an advisory capacity which was a great success. Long before your time I think. Can I put it to you both?"

"Put what?" This from Chloe.

He plunged. "I'd like you to come out to New Zealand to restore the big homestead. My television series makes it financially viable."

Chloe looked as if he'd taken her breath away. She closed her lips, swallowed, said, "Did I say my grandmother was a human dynamo? You must be her male counterpart. You must have some good firms over there. No need for this."

"But would I find anyone as inspired as this? Yes, they'd probably bring the motif of the First Four Ships in. I liked the Captain Scott touch, taking us back to 1911 and, not long after that, the capture of the gallant German sea captain Count von Luckner, who spent what he called 'long weary days of imprisonment' on Ripa Island in the harbour. A merciful man of the First World War, who never left men or even the ship's cat to drown when he captured their ships. I couldn't believe it when I saw you had incorporated that bit of history long before even your grandmother's time, I guess. It made me realise you must have read up the setting of my book in real earnest. No greater compliment could be given any author, finding out that someone other than himself had delved so deeply."

She suited the high colour it brought to her cheeks, the sparkle in her eyes. Leonora looked from one to the other and chuckled, "What makes you think this is so impossible, Chloe?"

More amazement. "Gran — no! When Dane comes to his senses he'll realise it's crazy. I know that years ago Elissa Montgomery went out to New Zealand, but then she'd spent her school years there when her mama was the governess to Rupert Airlie's children on that remote sheepstation, but Rupert Airlie engaged her for one reason only, he wanted to tempt her mother back again. I think you'd better have a good night's sleep, add up the cost, and forget it. Just look on this as a novel sort of signing session." She looked at Leonora to confirm this piece of good advice.

Leonora nibbled another luscious olive and declared, "I don't see why not! I've been wondering what sort of a reward I could give you for the three months' break you gave me in Canada. You succeeded in that task beyond all expectations. Take the offer, dear girl. I'll pay the travel costs, then you won't feel under an obligation."

Chloe was speechless. Her gaze met Dane's though. "Then that's settled," he said.

"Are all New Zealanders as impulsive as you?" she demanded.

"Not all," he admitted, "but a lot of us don't beat about the bush." And he went on to discuss the session details, as if it were a minor matter they had decided.

Dane asked, "Have you always been in the antique business, Leonora?"

Leonora nodded. "My very first job was as an assistant in an antique shop." She smiled as if at a pleasant memory. "I married the boss's son. This was in Newcastle upon Tyne. Our son runs it now. Chloe

44

grew up in the trade so ran this place while I was in Canada. What a good thing you hadn't taken up your job again, Chloe!"

Dane dropped asleep as soon as he got to bed, though Victoria and Blair wormed it all out of him, both intrigued.

Chloe lay awake a long time. She was surprised at that. What a day! Even the quarrel in the restaurant should have exhausted her. Losing your temper like that usually did. How could she have dreamed that before the day ended she would be planning a trip to the Antipodes? Till this afternoon Dane Inglethorpe had been just a name on the spine of his books, but now he was dominating her thoughts. Finally, contentedly, she fell asleep.

Dane thought the charm of Chloe's murals attracted the buying public as much as the advertisements, plus the novelty of this famous firm putting on a show like this. Leonora was surely a shrewd businesswoman. Not only were his sales benefiting, so were hers. However, he thought, it wasn't all business, as witness her generous offer of the air fare. He liked characters who were soft-hearted and vulnerable under their crusty exteriors. How would he describe her

45

if he had one like this in a future book? Not that he needed to use characters from real life. Most were composite types, inspiration springing from people met, but moulded into one's very own creation. Just a hint of the source — a certain characteristic, a way of speaking, possibly some revealing incident — could trigger off a whole book; a lot of research needed which brought you treasures undreamed of . . . the necessity for knowing more of your character's background — even early childhood — that would never be incorporated in any book, but gave you the insight into the depths and shallows within people. What was it about Leonora that intrigued him? Oh yes, he was far more intrigued about Chloe but he didn't need to analyse that! A reason as old as Eden. Man and woman. But he was aware that under the enamel-hard sophistication of the older woman, was something very vulnerable, some hurt he was sure she had triumphed over.

Dane shook himself free of this musing and entered into commercial dealing. It was very pleasantly surprising to have someone handing him three books she'd bought, sheer delight beaming from her eyes. She said: "Would you have time to autograph them rather personally? I mean to include the names of the recipients? Or —"

He smiled. "I sure can. A compliment to have you ready to give three copies away. Is there a story behind this? I mean are you sure each one reads this type of book?" She was almost middle-aged but there was real gladness in her eyes.

"Oh yes . . . they share kindred tastes. My husband, my mother, our daughter." Then she added, "For the first one would you put 'To Hugh from Sylvia, remembering a long-ago fifth of June'."

He looked at her and made an inspired guess. "Your wedding day?"

Her eyes widened. "Aren't you intuitive?" and went on to give the next inscription: 'To Mother, who taught me to read.' Finally 'To our daughter who is a kindred spirit.'

Dane was glad the queue had thinned out. He said with real warmth in his voice, "Thank you. Appreciation like this will often keep me at my desk, writing for readers like you — when I'm home again in New Zealand — on a day when I'd rather be out riding around the sheep on the hills above the bay. And I'll tuck your inscriptions away in a notebook, when this is over, and some day, you may find it in print, this incident. Nothing could be more pleasurable to an author than feeling he is supplying the reading needs of what amounts to a dynasty in the world of reading."

She sparkled, "Oh thank you, Dane Inglethorpe," picked up the books and her receipt and moved away to have them wrapped.

He encountered another pair of sparkling eyes, sea green, not blue. Chloe said delightedly, "Oh Dane, you've made her day . . . in fact probably her year!"

"I'd like to think so," he said. "Nice to meet up with a family like that, it warms the heart."

He caught sight of someone obviously wanting Chloe, not himself; handsome, elegant, keen. So he was surprised to hear her say, "Oh hullo Hudson. I think Leonora is in the inner room. Go on through will you? I'm rather too busy at the moment to get her."

Hudson! Not the creep he'd imagined!

Hudson shook his head. "It was you I wanted to see, of course, not Leonora. Though I want to see her about some stock she'll be interested in, in Middlesbrough. Great chance. Chap retiring. Shop needed for redevelopment." He dropped his voice. "Sorry about the other day. Stupid of me, but perhaps you could put it down to a certain eagerness." He sounded as if he were smiling. "But you could put it down to being really in love after all. So — how about giving me time in a more romantic setting? Give an inarticulate fellow another chance?"

Dane cursed inwardly at the inability of the moment to break this up. This guy certainly picked his times. Would this soften Chloe towards him?

Chloe's voice was of necessity discreet too, but he heard her say crisply, "Sorry, Hudson, but it was always out of the question . . . heart not involved you see. Besides, next month, or a little later, I'm off to New Zealand on a job, and excuse me, I see another wave of customers surging towards us. You know how important your business is to you. So is my business — or rather Leonora's business — to me. I'll have to see you in a commercial way until I leave, I know, but regard this as goodbye in a personal way — oh I see Gran's emerging with her customers and I must help Dane Inglethorpe with this next batch of eager beavers in the reading world."

The next moment, the first in the queue said to Dane: "I'm glad I didn't miss this. I do like to be in the swim. I can see you're the latest sensation and everyone will be asking me if I've read it."

Dane's eyes met Chloe's and somehow

neither of them laughed. He said in a quite kindly way, "Here you are, and I do hope you'll get around to reading it some time." Later, after a simple but enjoyable meal in the flat upstairs they had their laugh. "Nothing like signing sessions to cut you down to size," Dane said.

Chloe giggled. "I did like the incident with those two rather grubby little boys who appeared with their autograph books and said, 'This'll be the third important person we've got the signatures of'."

He grinned. "I had the sense not to ask who the other two were. Pity . . . it could have been the prime minister and a film star."

She looked mischievous. "I'm afraid I couldn't restrain my curiosity. I chased them to the door and asked."

"And?"

She chuckled. "Sorry to spoil your dream of entering the halls of fame in such celebrated company. One was our local boxer and the other was the butcher who made a name for himself recently by giving away free black puddings! His photo made the local paper."

Leonora decided it was time she served Dane her homemade apple pie.

He said with sincerity, "I hope Chloe can

make pie like this. In New Zealand everyone pitches in, especially during farm emergencies. I'll hope none lands her into what she'd probably consider a waste of her own artistic talents, but I must give her fair warning."

"Which reminds me," Leonora said, "we've not got down to tin tacks yet and we must. You mentioned two houses. What is the actual set-up young man, concerning my granddaughter?"

Chloe frowned. "Grandmama, what can you mean? This is the end of the century, not the beginning!"

Dane said swiftly, "I was going to see you about this, Leonora — my uncle and aunt keep house for me. It so happens they travelled over with me. Aunt was from Edinburgh originally and my uncle, though born in New Zealand, spent some time there and — in the old-fashioned term — won her heart. This trip they had planned for years. I rang them yesterday and mentioned what I have in mind. They're very glad for Phyl and Ross's sakes. I invited them to come to meet you as I knew this must crop up."

He looked very bland. "Their surname is Winchmore, and they are Uncle Joshua and Aunt Abigail."

Chloe looked at him across the table. "You are used to inventing names, aren't

51

you? So congratulations! They could hardly sound more conventional. Don't be such an idiot or you'll have my grandmother suspicious."

The heavy eyebrows flew up and he said mournfully, as if cut to the quick, "I hadn't realised the drawbacks of being an author. The things that befall you. Some accuse you of unreality, others that you are drawing upon fact and even more of plagiarising, quite forgetful that coincidences are always happening. Now I'm being accused of inventing mythical relations. I thought better of you, Chloe! How can I possibly add that Uncle Joshua is, in full, the Reverend Joshua Winchmore; the three years he spent in Britain were postgraduate studies at Oxford and he went to the Scottish Assembly in Edinburgh for one year to widen his ecumenical beliefs. Even in his younger days he sometimes took services in the small church old Aubrey built to serve the spiritual needs of his community."

Leonora burst out laughing. "Good for you, Dane. At my age I find it refreshing to know the younger generation can come such a cropper. Point taken. That's all I needed. When do we expect them?"

"The day after the last session. They'll stay with the Doigs. They know Blair's family in Central Otago — their favourite holiday place. Though occasionally they go to the far north — the Bay of Islands — where the first missionaries came. Chloe, after they get settled in with Victoria, if your grandmother can spare you, would you show me round some parts of Surrey I haven't yet visited? I have seen at least three of the manor houses or large estates Victoria tells me you've had a hand in restoring. Could you spare her, Leonora? I've got a lot of places I'd like to see yet, and to study."

"In a moment," said Chloe suspiciously, "you'll add that of course it's for purposes of authorship and I'm well aware you write only of New Zealand."

"Till now," he countered, "I've written only of New Zealand and New Zealanders, but I aim to branch out and am planning a heroine from this hemisphere."

She said, quite crossly, "I shall never know what you make up and what is reality."

"Oh this is for real. You can believe that." Once more their eyes met. Hers fell. His didn't.

She looked across at her grandmother with real concern showing. "Gran, I know you've got carried away with this link between the treasures that were bequeathed to you, and this particular book I lent you, but I'm not keen on you living here alone. Not only must we step up security but who is to keep an eye on you?"

"Your mother and father!" Leonora brought it out like a trump card. "Your father has had a very good offer for the business. It will be a wrench for them leaving Tyne and Wear, but he says if I could conquer my homesickness for the north, so can he and your mother. It's advantageous to us both; he'll bring down his surplus stock and of course he remembers so well the MacAlpines who were so good to me as a child. He'll love renewing acquaintance with my New Zealand room again. They both feel that this book of Dane's will have generated great interest in this South Pacific set-up, and now's the time to promote it with your following book appearing on TV so soon. Anything that brings customers in appeals to me."

Again Chloe wondered why Leonora didn't enlarge on her more personal interest. But it meant stirring up a sadness of the past. She'd always shown some reluctance to do that. Despite her business shrewdness her grandmother had a certain reticence in her which Chloe's mother had always suspected had to do with a small child, bereaved of both parents at an early age. Besides, she had a great respect for other people's need of privacy. Notwithstanding her great interest in the histories of the treasures she bought and sold, she was no gossip and never seemed to want to talk much about her own childhood. Well, that was over to her.

The Reverend Joshua and Abigail Winchmore proved a great success with everyone. Vicarage life over many years had given them an ease of manner and an ability to communicate well. Chloe, always interested in the stories behind the treasures of the antique shop — gathered from the four corners of the world — lapped it all up, and they in turn were fascinated with the older history all about them. Aunt Abbie, of course, was steeped in Scottish history, but she'd lived in New Zealand so long she too was versed in the century and a half and more of New Zealand's colonisation, and particularly of the Canterbury pilgrims as she called them, from the time of the arrival of the First Four Ships, and even before, when it was just a dream in the hearts of those who planned it, and braved the unknown.

Aunt Abigail may have had a no-nonsense

name but she was far from a plain Jane —
in fact, even at this age, she could be described as bewitching, with a kind of mature
loveliness of spirit as well as feature, and
Joshua was decidedly handsome. Not a
stereotype as one imagined vicars, but with
lines of crowsfeet etched at the corners of
his eyes, denoting a sense of humour. She
said as much to Dane but could have slain
him when he mentioned it to his uncle.
Joshua laughed. "I know — lots of folk harbour these ideas. An outspoken woman in
one of our parishes once said to me, 'We've
got used to you now. We'd heard you were
an acquisition to any church and imagined
you as saintly and beaming with a sort of
halo of piety clinging to you. Instead you're
just one of us.' As if I could be otherwise,
brought up in a farming family."

Chloe was interested. "Oh, I hadn't realised you came from a farming family too."

He nodded. "That's why the set-up at
Hauroko Bay is so ideal for us. Not only
did it save us investing our savings in a small
suburban house when I retired, but we live
in the old homestead I always loved — my
father's farm was just a run-of-the-mill estate out on the plains, but when Dane gets
married we're going to take over one of the
homes in old Aubrey's village. Needs a lot

doing to it naturally, but that would be a great project."

Chloe felt her interest stirring. She might be able to advise. She didn't put it into words. It might sound as if she was planning a longer stay than they would want . . . and it seemed as if there might be a love interest in Dane's life.

Joshua said, turning to Dane, "Which reminds me. We didn't fare any better than you did, in the matter of the long-ago offspring and subsequent heirs, even though we had more time than you. Perhaps just as well. You wouldn't really want anything cropping up now, with this new venture being embarked upon; could throw a spanner into the works. At one time it wouldn't have aroused much interest with the property suffering the slings and arrows of — perhaps not outrageous fortune — but the ups and downs of meat and wool markets."

Dane had a frown creasing his brows. "Yes — could be the best thing, but it leaves me feeling unsatisfied. Unfinished business. A bit stupid perhaps, in the circumstances. Perhaps it's the writer in me wanting to write a last chapter."

They were on their way to Portchester Castle at the time, something Dane and his aunt and uncle had dreamed of seeing for a long time and at that moment it came in sight. Chloe felt intrigued by this, though possibly it was private family business, so it remained a tantalising subject to ponder on. But then it was lost sight of in the fascination of exploring a place that had links with Roman times, and where Henry V, in 1415, set out on the expedition that was crowned with success at Agincourt.

In any case it couldn't matter to her, and the trip was only three weeks away, and it was going to be busy, settling Mother and Father into the new abode and business.

Chapter Three

To Chloe it seemed as if she were living in
a fantasy world. One moment she'd felt as
the immortal bard had said, that life was
flat, stale and unprofitable. Now she was
actually going off to New Zealand, with an
author whose books had delighted her for
so long . . . and Grandmother was pushing
it, and Mother and Dad, simply oozing ap-
proval. They must have been planning this
move for some time. Had probably had
Leonora on their minds as time had gone
by . . . she thought the trip Leonora had
taken to Canada had made them realise she
might be quite happy to relinquish some of
the responsibility now.

The last few weeks were hectic enough
but crammed with delightful happenings —
taking Dane to some of the choicest spots
in this lovely countryside; finding Joshua
and Abbie kindred spirits and great fun —
and it was only now and then a strange
regret touched her heart because it was going to be so fleeting — the incredible speed
of airliners that could whisk you from one

hemisphere to another — an enchanting glimpse of that fascinating setting Dane had revealed in his thriller about Hauroko, that bay where songs were borne on the winds of the Pacific Ocean. Well, she would be doing her own work for a few weeks and it seemed to her it would colour her whole life.

Then suddenly, they were actually airborne and looking down on the French Alps, sitting beside Dane and flying over unfamiliar territory . . . now they were sitting out a long wait at Singapore, incredibly fascinating with the sounds of the Near East, hot, colourful, crowded with milling throngs and with an incessant murmur of foreign tongues. Suddenly she saw two delightful imps of children, obviously getting up to mischief, and laughed out loud.

Dane turned to her. "What is it, Chloe?"

"Just that we seemed isolated by language and culture, but in a moment — like a flash — I could see my brother's children, and those parents look just as harassed as Ron and Sue do in similar circumstances." At that moment the little boy looked at her and grinned, a broad comradely grin. She smiled back.

"That's something to remember — all barriers down," Dane said, and fished for

60

the inevitable notebook. "Worth using in some book as yet undreamed of." She sat in silence, caught in the magic of knowing some day she might see this small incident in print. His tone seemed to change a little. "You have the most delightful laugh, Chloe, a tricksy laugh."

Chloe had a fleeting thought. Other men's compliments could seem very stale and trite after this man's! Which perhaps wasn't fair to less articulate males!

She saw his expression change and followed his gaze. Across what seemed like acres of bright carpeting a middle-aged woman was approaching. She was far enough off not to hear his suppressed groan as he turned to Joshua and Abbie and sighed, "Even here somehing crops up to disenchant us; trouble approaches — here's our Beatrice. What the hell's she doing here?"

She was extremely sleek, well-tailored, immaculate, dark with a lovely hairdo and her eyes sparkled as she greeted them. "What incredible luck — I do like company on a flight so when Merle rang me and said you were on this one too it seemed providential."

Chloe had an idea providential wasn't the word Dane would have used but he greeted her smoothly enough . . . Yes, smooth was the word, and when she offered a cheek to kiss, he didn't avoid it. She held out welcoming hands to Joshua and Abbie. Chloe noticed they relinquished them quickly, though they responded cordially enough. Nevertheless something was lacking.

Dane introduced them. "Beatrice, this is Chloe Lambard — whom I had the incredible luck to meet when her grandmother arranged a signing session for me in her shop in Surrey. She's giving this trip to Chloe because her granddaughter managed the shop for her while she took three months in Canada. Believe it or not, as she's an interior decorator she's going to transform the old homestead into — we hope — a very popular tourist attraction. We're all very keen. How many people would find such talent — someone with such fabulous colouring herself?"

Chloe was instantly aware of warmth in her cheeks. She had this odd feeling that he had something in his voice that reminded her of someone throwing down the gauntlet. That was absurd of course, but the two small curved lines at the corners of his mouth had deepened and she'd already observed that when he felt a strong emotion or wanted to laugh, this happened. A sort of devil-may-care expression. "Chloe, this is

Beatrice Brownlow who lives in the next bay to us. You'll probably see quite a lot of her."

Beatrice said, "Well, in the main I'll let Merle come over on her own. Her riding school is doing well, but perhaps we can swap seats around a little and Chloe could have mine while I tell you all you'll want to hear about Merle."

Chloe opened her lips to say 'Yes, of course' but Dane got in first. "Sorry Beatrice — can't be done. Chloe and I are spending most of our time this trip on discussing plans for the new venture. She's so good at sketching, it's marvellous to have the time uninterrupted by the telephone or doorbell. We've already accomplished quite a lot." And as he spoke he shifted what was on his knee beneath some magazines to conceal the cryptic crossword he and Chloe had been working on. The devil.

Chloe, bridging the moment, said, "I take it Merle is your daughter?"

"I wish I could agree. I look on her as my daughter; she's very dear to me. I live with them. A beautiful girl. Now she's a beauty in the classical style, perfect features. A painter who visited the harbour was quite lyrical about her profile. He thought her quite like one famous Grecian beauty of long ago."

"I don't wonder," said Abbie. "Her alabaster skin reminds me of some famous statue, can't remember who."

Chloe thought, Who'd want to be like a statue? — it sounded cold and remote. She was shocked at herself for hoping she was. Normally she'd have looked forward to meeting Merle.

They all went off to have coffee and some delightful Eastern concoctions to nibble, which made the conversation easier.

Beatrice dragged Merle and her activities in several times. The last time Dane said quite pleasantly, "Yes, she's been having fun . . . she told me of these doings when I phoned her last week."

Again, an out-of-character thought flashed into Chloe's mind. Having fun doesn't sound like a Greek goddess! Perhaps there's more to her than being statuesque, and a feeling of disquiet stirred something in her. She was only going out to do a job, wasn't she, *for so fleeting a time!*

"Did you have any luck in that other matter?" Beatrice said to Dane. "Though hardly likely after all these years, and much better if you didn't. Might mean a cuckoo in the nest. Even a threat. I still can't understand why you wanted to pursue the hunt."

Again Chloe saw the lines deepen, but

not with laughter. His voice was suave though. "Let's just say it would satisfy something in me — perhaps it's ingrained in an author to want to unravel an unfinished story."

"Probably," said Beatrice more comfortably, "that'll be it."

"And a certain integrity and a sense of fair play," Joshua interjected.

Dane grinned, at ease once more. "You make me sound a paragon and nobody really likes paragons — so cut it out, Uncle Josh."

At that moment their call came. They were travelling business class and Dane, rather ostentatiously, arranged their sketches and photographs on the neat worktable between them. They knew they'd soon be settling down for the night but a delicious meal was served first. Dane took a quick look along the aisle to where Beatrice was ensconced, saw with satisfaction she was getting served first with her blanket and pillow, and took out their crossword.

Chloe chuckled — a chuckle that was hardly more than a whisper — and said, "Why do I feel like a pupil in a classroom, with one of your books hidden under an English paper?"

"Oh, come off it Chloe — you'd finished

with school long before my first book appeared."

Her eyes sparkled. "You ought to have said 'Of course — you'd just be a schoolgirl'."

His eyes glinted. "I don't want you to be too young. You'll have noticed my heroines are never teenagers — I like my women mature. What age are you? I'd say twenty-five or six."

"How very astute! Twenty-five last birthday."

"I'm thirty-four — how does that strike you? As fairly old?"

She had a mad desire to reply 'Just right!' Whatever had come over her? She *must* rid herself of this feeling that the world was a more enchanting place than it used to be.

By the time they finished their crossword almost everybody was settling down and those who weren't had earphones clamped to their heads and the screen at one end was flickering. "Can't understand wanting to watch a film," she said drowsily.

"I've no wish to either — but some can't sleep on a plane. Can you? Or haven't you had the experience?"

"Oh, I had a holiday in Canada before Gran did and slept well — a shorter trip of course — and I had no jet lag."

"Good girl." Then he laughed. He tapped the desk-like table between them. "Much more comfy than jammed in between people, of course, but it has one drawback."

"What's that?" asked Chloe innocently.

"Just that it wouldn't have bothered me one bit to find your head on my shoulder in the morning."

"You sound like one of your own books — I guess it's a habit. Don't be stupid," she remarked, hiding a smile.

He laughed, turned out their light and, after a quick look across the aisle at his uncle and aunt, leaned across and kissed her, fleetingly.

"Good night. Sleep well and pleasant dreams."

Chloe knew she mustn't make too much of it. No doubt authors were susceptible creatures. She closed her eyes as if still drowsy though instead she felt her pulses quicken. Behind the barrier of her eyelids she told herself not to be foolish — it was just that she found herself bowled over by having her favourite author kiss her so unexpectedly. Probably a romantic and fleeting feeling after the prosaic Hudson! She must discipline herself, remembering these people lived their lives in another hemisphere. She and Dane were like ships that passed in the night. Now, who said that? She drifted over the threshold of sleep, content, relaxed.

She had a lovely dream — in it she saw volcano-green waters like those described to her, with gentle bays cutting back into hills that were often parched and brown, like he had said. The contours seemed familiar — even in her dream. She knew it was partly because of Dane and partly those drawings she had known by heart so long. The names of the features flashed into her subconscious, names full of imagery — Castle Rock, Witch Hill, the Giant's Causeway — and what was the name of that restored rest-house that looked down onto the harbour at one side, and on the other — across the vast stretch of plain that spread, he'd said, from the fringes of Christchurch across sixty miles to the Southern Alps — a great chain of mountains running north and south, with, on its far side, a narrow strip they called the West Coast. How fascinating to know that the east coast was pounded by the Pacific Ocean, and on the West, the Tasman Sea that divided New Zealand from the great land mass of Australia.

She woke suddenly, sure the night was over. The cabin was dim, hushed. She looked up to find Dane looking down on her. Their eyes met in a long, recognising exchange. A strange look as if they searched and found. He had a little smile playing around his lips, as if he had liked the tenor of his thoughts. She wondered if he roamed in some fictitional meadow of his own fancy. But somehow it was a moment shared.

Suddenly she felt self-conscious and said the first thing that flashed into her mind. Her voice was little more than a whisper. "How odd — your eyebrows look older than the rest of you!"

He gave an involuntary chuckle. "Why, for goodness' sake?"

"They are bushy. The rest of you is so smooth, so suave. As if you're by nature almost gentle and dreamy, but any moment, if you lost your temper, they could give you the look of a real curmudgeon."

He whispered back, "You are going to be an inspiration — I can see that. One of the golden rules in character drawing is to have some small defect — it's sort of endearing. Perfection in description can be irritating. A quirk in features or character makes fiction spring to life."

Unbidden the thought of Merle's classical beauty sprang to mind.

She smiled and said, "What a very odd conversation to have in the middle of a night flight. Have you been awake long?"

"I haven't been to sleep at all. Seemed a waste."

"That's what comes of being an author, and I suppose you need your thinking time, to ponder on a plot."

"We'll put it down to that," he answered smiling. "Now goodnight once more and here's hoping you can dream again the dream that made you smile in your sleep like a child." He closed his eyes and was instantly asleep she was sure. She drifted off again.

They woke to a cabin astir with stewards and stewardesses bustling about with hot steaming facecloths to refresh the passengers and the sound of trays rattling for breakfast.

"Some poor sleepers, no doubt, are saying '*What* a night!'"

Dane's tawny eyes twinkled as they met hers. "I could say that too, with a different inflection, thank you, Chloe." She didn't know what he was thanking her for.

Dawn was streaking a cornflower blue sky with rose and gold as they cruised above the clouds, and a light somehow different from any other sky she'd seen. She said so. He nodded. "We must be nearing Australia. I've an artist friend who says the light is quite different from New Zealand. Very fascinating to capture on canvas. As if the vastness of it catches the sun. New Zealand looks, on maps, like a squiggle beside it yet it's the size of England and Scotland put together, but much less populated of course. In New Zealand our skies have many more cloudscapes for artists to draw but a more temperamental weather pattern. Soon after breakfast, if there's a break in the cloud, you'll see the shining beauty of Sydney Harbour and the immense spread of a glorious city. I think I told you we came via Australia so we could land in Christchurch, close to home. If you go by the United States and Los Angeles, you come into Auckland, another lovely harbour; in fact twin harbours. The City of Sails they call it."

"I know — you had it in *Fear not Tomorrow*, at least two chapters. Ah — here's our breakfast."

Another voice, Joshua's, chimed in across the aisle. "And I'm ready for it. I love not knowing what we'll get. Did you two sleep well?"

Again the smooth, meaningful inflection in Dane's voice. "We passed a delightfully relaxed night." His eyes met Chloe's, glancing down at her.

"I suppose this is all copy to you — grist to the author's mill?" she said wryly.

"You could put it that way," he agreed. "Ah, the incomparable aroma of coffee — after travelling halfway round the world; three-quarters in fact."

After the meal everyone showed excitement. Some were leaving the plane at Sydney, and as they were descending on a course for the runway, Chloe thought, what a coastline. How much there was of it — far as the eye could see, and fringed with an ocean of cobalt blue.

"But when we reach home," Dane told her, "New Zealand will be living up to its true name — Aotearoa, the 'Land of the Long White Cloud'. Just as those magnificent Maori explorers saw it, so long ago, from their canoes."

"Don't you want to jot that down?" asked Chloe. "Otherwise it could escape you. I'd like to meet it in a book sometime when I'm back in England. You might forget that turn of phrase if you don't write it down."

"I don't need to. It's part of my early years. I was brought up on those stories. New Zealand didn't just begin with the advent of the Pakeha you know — with the coming of the white man; the European."

A sense of expectancy of new knowledge awaiting her, a breath of adventure, a time of magic perhaps — again that quickening

of the pulse, a feathering of excitement —
assailed Chloe's mind and senses.

The magnificence and beauty of Sydney
Harbour lay beneath them, as the plane
circled in towards the runway, contoured as
if God had loved fashioning it; the shining
span of the bridge, the winged whiteness of
the Opera House jutting out into waters so
colourful they could be an artist's palette,
and all about it that shimmering haze of
light. A new world! But not her own dear
world.

Dane asked, "Did we mention New Zealand is two hours ahead of Australia? The
sun touches the east coast of the North
Island first, fingering it lovingly, and adding
a golden quality to the grapes grown there.
Though I believe the Chatham Islands now
truly claim that sunrise distinction and the
new millenium will be marked there.
They're small islands to the east of Christchurch, sparsely populated. And we are pa-
rochial enough to be glad Captain Cook
discovered us first, then sailed on to discover
Australia. Our side of the harbour is part of
Banks Peninsula, named for his great naturalist, Joseph Banks; they thought it was an
island at first."

"That I do know," said Chloe smugly.

"After reading one of your books I hunted up his findings in the museum."

Dane's eyes looked into hers. "You're the sort of reader I can really appreciate — an informed reader. When I saw an early map of those newly charted waters pinned up on your wall, I knew you for someone after my own heart."

Joshua leaned across and remarked, "Sounds like a history and geography lesson to me. When I was a young man I found other things to interest beautiful girls. You've no technique, nephew!"

Abbie cut in. "Just hark at him — the man whose idea of courtship was to take me mountaineering. Me! I was terrified of heights. I didn't think I could stand the pace."

Joshua chuckled. "Yes — but I wooed you with Robert Browning's and Herrick's passionate love poems as well as the outdoors."

What a couple they were — made you believe in love!

"We're dipping down," said Dane.

What a fabulous airport, thought Chloe, with some fascinating duty-free shops. The three of them bought her some delightful items. Inwardly she pulled a face; the sort of things you bought as souvenirs for short-term visitors. Beatrice clung like a limpet. It was afternoon when the flight took off again.

"But it will be later in Christchurch-on-the-Avon," said Joshua, "as long ago Sir Anthony Eden called it." Then he added: "But though it has the name of being our most English city, it's not named after Shakespeare's Avon but a Scots river in Lanarkshire."

"Who's being the pedant now?" grinned Dane.

Then a perfect view condensed into one enchanting glimpse, the visibility so good as they flew beneath the cloud cover, they saw it like a relief map shore to shore . . . Stewart Island, very tiny, in the far south, the narrow Westland strip, the "Long White Cloud" above that breathtaking chain of mountains, topped by Mount Cook; the sweep of the plains to the east with huge riverbeds and lakes draining the snow and glaciers on each side, and the momentary glimpse of a fretwork of sounds at the extreme northern tip of the South Island and, as Dane pointed out, the treacherous waters of Cook Strait, one of the most feared and respected stretches of water in the world; and with the North Island across it, Dane proudly pointing it out, grateful for the amazing miles of visibility.

Then they were circling round and dipping down. Chloe had a fleeting impression of high-rise buildings, a city laid out with the Roman precision like some English cities — Chichester for one — and a square mile of inner city bounded by four avenues named after the early colonists and explorers she knew: Fitzgerald, Moorhouse, Bealey and Rolleston.

"Let's not hustle things," said Dane, "after all we're not in transit any more — we're home." There was an exultancy in his voice.

Beatrice appeared at their side. "Not long now, dear boy," she remarked, "and you'll see her."

Then they were through customs and in the arrival lounge. People separated into groups, some on conducted tours.

Then Chloe saw her. This couldn't be other than the Greek goddess . . . statuesque, enchantingly lovely with wheat-gold hair lying in smooth curls on her forehead, a lovely line of chin and a truly classical nose. Dane put down his briefcase and held out both hands to her. A light flashed in those dark blue eyes. She lifted her face for his kiss. "Hello, Blackbird," he said. "Hello, Great Dane," she replied. Chloe caught a quick question he asked her. "All well with you, Merle?" A serene smile curved her lips. She said, "Yes, now all is well."

Chloe had a sense of anticlimax. She was fascinating as well as beautiful and there was no doubt they were good pals. 'Blackbird' was the meaning of her name. Other greetings followed. Josh and Abbie seemed delighted to see her too.

"Well, Aunt Bea," said Merle. "Have you got the travel-bug out of your system yet?" Beatrice smiled rather provocatively. "Not really. Maybe it's just whetted my appetite for more. But I must see *you* settled first."

Something of the shining splendour of the day dimmed a little for Chloe.

Chapter Four

Merle said, "Pity we knew so late that Bea was coming on this plane too — I could have brought the station wagon. I rang Hauroko and Phyl told me Ross was coming with his. Phyl got a ring from the council in Christchurch re the development in the bay, so had to stay home. She would rather you had been there but the powers-that-be, after all this time, made it today — sheer ill luck."

Dane's brows twitched together. "I'd rather it had been next week when I'm sure they'd have been impressed with what Chloe and I are planning. She's even taken my mind off my next book."

"No wonder," smiled Merle warmly, "a girl like this!"

So she wasn't mean-spirited or jealous of this stranger coming into their midst. Perhaps she had no need to fear a rival. Chloe shook her mind free of these disturbing thoughts . . .

Ross arrived. "I suppose it's straight home now Dane?"

He nodded, "I'm dying to see the bay

again . . . By rights we ought to take Chloe through Christchurch first so her initial impression is of a city built round its cathedral and see the direct line of Colombo Street leading south to the hills, but —"

Chloe said eagerly, "I'm all for the shortest way, lead on." The luggage came through and they moved off. She had an impression of a widely spreading plains city, and beyond it, grey hills guarding and sheltering it in a magnificent curve.

"We go up and over them to our own harbour," said Abbie.

As they left the flatness behind Chloe saw a structure that caught her eye. "That could be anywhere in England!" she exclaimed. "What is it?"

"That was designed and built by a man who'd never seen England," Dane told her. "Took him years and in the face of much opposition. Harry Ell — still remembered as 'Harry Ell of the Summit Road'. It's called The Sign of the Takahe, the first of the chain of rest-houses he envisaged to circle the hills which would attract trampers."

Then they left the residential area of the lower slopes and the road swept on and up. They came to the Sign of the Kiwi on the crest, another stone edifice. Ross drew to a stop. "I believe Dane wants you to see the view from here — across to the mountains in the west, and to see the whole sweep of Pegasus Bay on the east and then to look down on the harbour — a perfect day for it."

Chloe's gasp as she gazed, and her resultant silence, were tributes in themselves. Then Dane swung her round and there it lay, sea-green, sparkling in the late afternoon sunlight, contoured in headlands and bays.

She said, "But this is more intimate, more individual."

"Good sentence," approved Dane.

Ross laughed. "We'd better warn you, Chloe, that anything you say may be taken down and used against you. We're used to living with an author. You may not be, so watch your every word."

"I'm being maligned," said Dane. "People regard authors with suspicion. Makes some people unnatural, though I doubt if Chloe comes into that category. She has a most disturbing yet endearing habit of saying whatever flashes into her mind at the moment."

"You make me sound someone to be afraid of," Chloe laughed.

"But she isn't," said Joshua. "She suits this family. No humbug, no guile."

She flushed. "Oh Joshua, you say the nicest things."

Dane spread his hands out in a gesture of resignation. "I'm being outclassed by my uncle. When I say those things she regards me with distrust — thinks I'm practising dialogue — as if I'd kissed the Blarney Stone. But Josh's dog-collar puts him above reproach, like Caesar's wife!"

"Well, it might at that," said Joshua, "if I was wearing it! Dashed uncomfortable things and, besides, some folks steer clear of the clergy."

"You two sound like bickering children," Abbie chided them. "You stopped here to show Chloe the view."

Chloe had turned from those sea-green waters to look westward and said, "Look at the sky above the Alps — it's celadon green and despite that heavy one way up, there isn't a cloud, not even a tiny one. I've never seen a sky like that. Does it mean rain?"

"That's a forerunner of our famous nor'wester," said Dane, "clever of you to notice. Not rain, a hot dry wind. Not that it starts that way. It comes across the Tasman full of moisture, drops it on the Alps and the wind pushes up the clouds like a theatre curtain, then next day roars across the plains. Mid-Canterbury is the dustbowl of that rich area and while it is a curse when you're stacking hay and it gets blown across the road against the neighbours' pine trees, it's also a blessing; their sheep never get footrot!"

"More geography," complained Joshua.

Dane grinned. "I save my more poetic utterances for the times when you are not around."

Ross cut in. "By now Sarah will be dancing with frustration, sure the plane is delayed, and afraid she won't be able to reveal her great surprise for you. Pip will wait till she gets you to herself. Now for the Question Mark Road down to Governor's Bay — the cherry blossom is beginning to show."

They had tussocky hills on their right and on their left a gully of native bush where small cascades took their way down to the sea below. Chloe turned to Dane. "Is that where your heroine fled, heart in mouth, from tree to tree, and the birds hushed their singing?"

The sea-green eyes were as sparkly as the waters of Diamond Harbour.

The hills were much greener this side, less exposed to a sun that could be merciless. As they reached the shore road, the first bridal transparency of the cherry blossom greeted them and underneath the trees

Chloe glimpsed a wave of daffodils. So springtime came to this hemisphere a little like her own dear corner back home!

Dane pointed. "See! They run right up that bank. The bride who came here a hundred years ago planted them and called it Daffodil Hill. We have some under our orchard trees too."

What an indented coastline. She was prepared for that, of course, from those old sketches. Long arms of land ran out into the sea, and she recognised Quail Island where long ago was a leper colony. But now the miracle of modern medicine had set the sufferers free of that fear. They had gone to another island, far off in the Pacific, where Father Damien had lightened their loneliness, and cures were found. There were always some people who moaned about the 'good old days', forgetting that not all was good . . .

The road was all dips and twists, following the contours. There were some exquisite homes and gardens along it, colourful in their springtime garb. This was what they called the Head of the Harbour. They passed dozens of hikers who all waved. Then they curved around to run east again. "What a place this must be for artists and poets," Chloe exulted.

Dane was moved by this. It showed in his voice. "I must take you to see our grandmother. You would delight her. She wrote poetry. Oh, other things too, articles and short stories, but she was at her best with poetry. Still is."

Chloe turned an astonished face to his. "Oh, is your grandmother still alive? Oh, how silly of me. No reason why she shouldn't be, but knowing your parents are both gone, I hadn't expected this. My own great-grandmother wrote poetry though I only just remember her. But her poetry lives on in her scrapbooks and Leonora used to read it to us when we were younger. Where is your grandmother? Fairly near?"

"It always seemed to us she and Grandfather lived 'over the hills and far away'. We loved them so much. Mother's parents. But distance grows shorter the longer you live and it's no distance really, about thirty-five miles south from Cathedral Square. Mid-Canterbury. That's where I remember the haystack blown across the road. We stayed with them for a few weeks once and had to go to Ashburton High School. We travelled eighteen miles each way by school bus and I well remember this farm on the main road cutting their hay in idyllic weather as we passed. We were so puzzled when their haystack couldn't be seen on our return, till the driver pointed out these dark pines and blue-gums, planted as great shelter belts on the far side, all festooned with what had been meant to feed their sheep that winter."

They began to pass through several small bays, secluded and fascinating, with small boats bobbing at their moorings, then they turned into Hauroko Bay. They didn't need to say 'Here we are' for there were the homestead buildings, and running back into the crotch of the hills what was unmistakably the deserted village between its avenue of English trees. It was all so familiar to Chloe, growing up as she had done, with Leonora's New Zealand room. Sheep dotted the hillsides, the sun shone on the gleaming russet coats of Hereford cattle, and the sunset was gilding the windows.

Ross sounded a gay tattoo on his horn and the place immediately sprang to life; dogs barked, doors opened and figures appeared, two smaller ones in the lead. Ross said apologetically, "I'm afraid you'll be put in the shade, Chloe, till Sarah gasps out her news. Best to get it over with."

Sarah looked about eleven, with long, swinging fair plaits; the smaller, Pip, about eight, darker, pixie-ish yet somehow very like her uncle.

Sarah gasped out her news, to outdo any-one getting in first, "We wanted to do some-thing to celebrate your coming home, Dane — but we didn't have to. Hildegarde did it for us just yesterday. She had her foal then — a filly — and *I* helped at the birth. Merle supervised of course and she said I did well."

Dane caught her up, kissed her, said, "Well done. And as soon as we've sorted ourselves out, we'll be off to the paddock." His hand went down to take Pip's. "And what have you got to tell me, poppet?"

Her dress had a long skirt to it and huge pockets. She dived into one and brought it out, a dead starfish, perfectly shaped, bright orange. "But I haven't found a sea horse yet," she mourned.

Chloe stooped down. "Oh, Pip, this makes me feel right at home. I come from Tyneside and part of our city's coat-of-arms is of a sea horse. Maybe we'll find one together." The little face lit up.

Phyl was lovely in manner and features. She greeted her brother and said ruefully, "I'm afraid the charms of the foal have quite eclipsed your homecoming, Dane, and Chloe will feel ignored. Quite an afternoon — I was wishing you were here but every-thing seems to be approved as long as we take out adequate insurance and obey fire safety precautions. The group included someone from the Tourist Board and his enthusiasm swayed the others, I think. But some tea first and a later dinner which will be here of course. I feel in a happy daze, my dream coming true at last. Chloe, you're an answer to our prayers, and what a wonderful thing that you and your grandmother already knew so much about this setting from your colonial treasures, and then Dane's books. And he tells me that one of the sketches actually included the village houses that were sold and removed later. Will you be able to reproduce them? Dane tells me you are no mean artist yourself. It would add to the atmosphere."

Dane assured her that Chloe already had her own sketch of that era, in her folio.

The homestead was beautiful, firing Chloe's imagination, reminiscent of another age when settlers, homesick for all they had left behind, created something as near as possible to the old dear familiar things. There was grandeur in every inch . . . the archways, the inset windows, the elegant staircase, well lit from a lancet window on the landing. Far too big a house, of course, for a family of four, and expensive to keep up, with farming at a low ebb in terms of markets and tariffs, so it was no less than wonderful that Dane's books could provide the wherewithal to retain it as it deserved. The ballroom where once they had danced in crinolines and bustles, was to be the restaurant and the windows on three sides gave enchanting glimpses of the harbour, right to the Heads . . . a big container ship was entering it at that very moment. There was another view of that village street, and over to one side another house, the old homestead presumably, much smaller but with a charm of its own, with wide, spreading verandahs and a quaint sort of tower on top, open to the sky and well-railed.

Dane followed her gaze. "There's a little stairway leads up to that — a great place to watch the shipping coming in, especially when it was under sail, bringing news from 'Home' and commodities they sorely needed."

"And books," said Phyl, "and sheets of music. They brought pianos with them, and fiddles. The piano in the drawing room is an original one."

The dinner was superb. Phyl's overseas experience in catering had certainly made her ideal for this . . . Chloe found herself hoping that *she* never had to step into her shoes in any of these emergencies Dane had spoken of. It was hardly likely she could reach this standard.

Over coffee Phyl said, "I know you must all be dying to get over to your own quarters. The girls have promised not to expect a story about England tonight."

Dane grinned. "I know. They were at pains to tell me that, so I compromised by promising them two tomorrow night. The light has almost gone so come on, folks. Ross, what are you looking up in that dictionary?"

"A word I'd never heard before till Chloe used it this afternoon, looking at that nor'west sky. It was celadon. Beats me. She could be a great help to you with your books, Dane."

Phyl said hurriedly, "She's here to work for me — not be a secretary."

"Oh, but she's a girl of many parts." Dane chuckled, "I've got to confess I looked it up too, surreptitiously. Wondered how she knew it but when I saw the meaning I realised it was to do with her antique training. It's a pale green Chinese glaze. So I didn't feel so much of a peasant after all." They all laughed.

Ross said, "It's good to see you being humble — now me, I'm just a horny-handed son of the soil."

Dane said affectionately, "Humbug . . .

no one who reads as deeply as you do could be that. Wasn't Robbie Burns a son of the soil? Well, that's it — we won't be long before we hit the hay. I take it you've got the larder well stocked over there, dear sister?"

"Of course," said Phyl, "as if you needed to ask. And flowers in the vases as well I can guarantee."

That was evident. The perfume of violets and narcissi greeted them as they entered the old homestead. "This is a darling house," said Chloe, "small, intimate, lacking the magnificence of the second homestead, but full of graciousness somehow."

Her three companions looked immensely gratified. Joshua gave her a hug. "I thought that as you're used to marble halls and stately homes hundreds of years old, this might seem rather paltry to you."

Her eyes were shining. "I find the fact that this one's history is quite recent most endearing. How old is it, about a hundred and eighty years? Then its history is telescoped into just a few generations." Her eyes swept round the smaller rooms, the lower ceilings, observing. "This ceiling looks like metal, painted over. Is that possible? The rest are beamed."

"Clever," said Dane. "It's rather unique.

The room above has the same. Quite a prosaic reason — at first it was roofed with *totara* shingles and a patch of them lifted, letting rain in, and old Aubrey acquired this from somewhere or other. There were some houses shipped out, that we'd call prefabricated these days. I guess the wily old beggar persuaded some settler hard pressed for ready money, to part with it. The room above is your room — one of the dormers. When I phoned Phyl from England I told her to get it ready for you."

"Why this one?"

"Because it's an end one, so has two views, one of Abbie's old-fashioned cottage garden, and one of the beach below."

They showed her over the rest of it. At the sight of a wide, low bed in their room, Abbie gave a happy sigh. "That's the best sight of all."

"There's nothing quite so comfy as your own bed, is there?" Chloe remarked.

"Oh it's not that," said Abbie, "it's just that so many of the bed and breakfast places we stayed in over in Britain, had twin beds and after all these years being married I do miss cuddling up to Joshua."

Joshua spread his hands out in what was now a familiar gesture to Chloe and said to Dane, "Did you say Chloe was apt

91

to speak whatever flashed into her mind? Well, that makes two of them."

"Consider yourself lucky, dear uncle. Some women are so reticent they lack warmth and feeling. I never have them in my books."

"Yes, true enough, but it sometimes made life in a vicarage less than circumspect. Some of our parishioners were continually being surprised."

Chloe came to Abbie's rescue. "But I guarantee they loved her just the same, even as I do."

Abbie flushed but there was pleasure written on her face. There was a white cotton knitted spread on the bed in her room and one in Chloe's too. "Is it possible these were made in the very early days?"

Abbie nodded. "They came out on the sailing ship Aubrey and his Caroline took passage on, very soon after their wedding." She stroked theirs. "It has seen many bridals and births."

"A happy house," said Chloe, and yawned.

"Time we were all in bed," stated Dane.

"But I've not seen where you write," Chloe protested.

"Plenty of time for that," he reminded her, "all the days ahead."

It was her last conscious thought, a blissful thought, as she tumbled into bed . . . not a hasty stay.

She woke to a glorious morning, New Zealand springtime at its best, though Dane warned her it could be as capricious as an English April. It was wonderful to hear and recognise familiar birdsongs: thrushes and blackbirds whistling, sparrows twittering; now and then the raucous sound of magpies. She saw one fly away from high up in an Australian gum. They seemed to have less white than their English counterparts . . . then she heard a different birdcall. This was like a chime of bells, as if it was being allowed to fall in tune with the little brook that cascaded gently on its winding way through this very garden.

She left the window, showered, slipped into green jeans and a top that matched her eyes, tied the red hair back in a ponytail, changed her mind and plaited it instead, tossing it back over her shoulder, and then ran down the old stairway to be greeted by an aroma of frying home-cured bacon over which Joshua was presiding. He had a big blue and white striped apron on and was telling Dane to crack the eggs. They swung round. She said, "Is Abbie suffering from jet lag? Do let me help."

Joshua smiled indulgently, "No, not her. She's out feeding the birds, scared they'll not come after so long an absence. They usually wait in ranks. So she's calling them — listen."

Abbie came in, those blue eyes sparkling.

"You'll have to put a new top on the bird table, Josh, that one is splitting. I'll put some jam and water out for the bellbirds and tuis and wax-eyes on the old stump, later."

"Was that what I heard?" asked Chloe, "how very apt. Just like a chime of bells."

"Later you'll hear a tui — it mimics the bellbird a lot except the bellbird never achieves its twanging note, a sort of sweetly harsh sound, as if its wings had brushed a woodland harp in passing. You'll recognise the tui by two tufts of white feathers under its chin; that's why they call it the parson bird, and by the way, the Maori name for the bellbird is the *Koromiko*."

The green eyes lit up. "Are there good prints of these native birds, in colour? I could do with some to go underneath each other in those narrow strips between the taller ballroom windows, as a change from the colonial historical ones."

"We've even got some," said Dane, "in my study, including one or two originals.

I'll take you in there soon as we've finished. Then you're to see the new filly. I persuaded the girls last night that they'd have to wait till today; thought it might be too much for you. They'll be here soon so let's go into the study now."

As soon as she entered Chloe knew a sense of awe. She said so. "To think so much creation has taken place here. How could I have dreamed when I read your first book that I'd ever be standing in the study it was conceived in, to say nothing of the hours of labour bringing it to birth? It's like hero-worshipping for ages, then meeting the hero."

He chuckled. "One never sees oneself as a hero, you dope! Just an ordinary person, and — as you'll see by my garb this morning — a farmer."

True he looked more rugged than the author who'd been talking to her grandmother when she'd first beheld him in the flesh, so soon after losing her temper with Hudson. He was wearing a loudly-checked Swan-dri shirt loose over well-worn jeans, sleeves rolled up on muscular forearms.

His study was extremely workmanlike with *rimu* bookshelves built all round it, a golden-brown, native timber, good lighting, and a long desk that held a word processor, fax machine and a copier. Then an older desk that had probably belonged to his grandfather, she thought, with a shabby leather inset and deep drawers, wide enough in the top to take book-troughs within hand-reach of the chair.

"That's older than the colonial era, isn't it?" Chloe said.

He nodded. "Sure is — believe it or not, it belonged to Aubrey. Came out on a sailing ship. They had a rough time near the Azores — got damaged a bit, I'll show you; I'm attached to these dents and scratches. I call that my inspirational desk. Even to sit at it stirs the muse — prods it wide awake."

She ran her hands lovingly along the edge. "And so it should. Oh — I hear the children."

They came racing headlong down the Dip as they called the incline from the other property.

"Built when this was raw and new, Chloe, and shelter was so desirable from the contours of the land, till their trees grew. The land had been cleared too vigorously, you see, for pasture, which ruined a lot of the native bush. But, of course, the timber was needed for the houses. No conservation societies then. They learned by their mistakes and were slow to learn at that."

The girls burst in. "We're all going up to see the mare and foal now and we've a surprise for Chloe. It's to mark her arrival here. Dad's idea . . . Chloe is to have the honour of naming the filly."

Chloe flushed with pleasure, then protested, "But I'm sure you already had a name picked out for her."

Pip nodded gravely, "But Dad said it was a daft one, more like a nursery rhyme — so, wait till you see her."

They all took off and stood enchanted to see the little foal with almost black glistening skin, running beside her mother.

Sarah was impatient, "Did you think of a name coming up the hill Chloe?"

Chloe had. "Just tell me one thing, Sarah, is it customary to have a string of foals all bearing the same initial letter?"

Sarah considered that. "Yes . . . not always, but Merle does with hers, though she'll run out of names before long. Her brood mare is Zillah, you see, and not many names begin with Z."

"Then she'll have to invent new names," said Pip, sensibly, "though I like well-known names best and knowing how to pronounce them."

"Well?" urged Sarah.

"As her mother is Hildegarde, let's call

her Heloise," Chloe suggested.

"Well done," said Dane. "Both of Teutonic origin."

Chloe turned an astonished face to him. "How could you possibly know that?"

He grinned. "I think all authors study names and meanings. Have to or else they find all their characters have names starting with the same initial and if they persist in using them some poor printer gets mixed up. Worst I ever saw was when a guy who was aspiring to write a novel asked me to give an opinion. There were four names in the first chapter, Angus, Agnes, Alice and Allan. When I pointed this out he renamed some and they immediately took on much more individual characteristics."

Chloe said, "But your characters seem to fit their names perfectly. You must study some excellent reference book."

He chuckled, "You'll see it in the study. A small booklet called *What to call the Baby*. I left it across at Phyl's one day and Ross leapt to the wrong conclusion when he saw it on her kitchen table. Thought they were about to hear the patter of tiny feet once more."

"Gosh!" said Sarah. "That would throw a spanner in the works just now, wouldn't it? I mean how could she go ahead with this plan if she had a baby?"

"No idea!" laughed Dane. "You'd better warn her off. But in private, mind. And anyway, look at Heloise. Talk about grace in motion." Then the men decided it was more than time they rode round the sheep. Dane said to Chloe, "You won't feel deserted and strange, will you?"

All part of his charm she thought, so she said with sincerity, "I'm not likely to feel that way. I'm dying to get Phyl to myself and get on with what I came here for. I always lose myself in work and with this setting I'm brimming with ideas. Off you go."

He grinned. "I think you're going to have a couple of hangers-on trailing after you." His gesture indicated the girls. "They might have some jolly good ideas," she retorted, "which I might be able to deal with better than yours."

"I'm squashed," said Dane, "come on, Ross."

Phyl was glad to have this interior decorator to herself, apart from the children. Chloe took her folio over and they seemed to inspire each other. They decided on a touch of green to repeat the colour of the harbour waters for the restaurant.

"Like your eyes," said Phyl. "They really

are just as Dane said — a pure translucent green like our bay."

"When did he say that? Of course I expect all authors are like this, they've got to describe characters so often. As if they'd kissed the Blarney Stone!"

"I've never known my brother quite so lyrical. And he said it in a letter. I might add, since you seem to have such doubts about the sincerity of his compliments, I've never known him like this — and he's been writing books some years now." She laughed. "He told me Miles Burford asked him to pep up the love interest and it surely shows."

Chloe shrugged, "Well it's all grist to the mill, I dare say. But I doubt if he'll want a ginger-headed heroine. Not everyone likes carroty hair."

Phyl was horrified. "Carroty? Hardly — in this morning sunlight it's like one of our newly-minted commemorative dollars."

"I'm beginning to think you should write books, too. Look, I brought these swatches of material from a firm we've used a lot, finding out first from the manufacturers if they were obtainable in New Zealand. By good luck their agency is in Christchurch."

"Oh, how wonderful — see that rosebed banked against that stone fence these windows look out on? The ones at the back have the sweetest scent of all, they're apricot and cream, and the lower row in front are apricot Vesper — those ones that stay as rosebuds longer than any. You'll see them in bloom in November and again in their second blooming in February."

Chloe laughed. "The redecorating won't take me as long as that, Phyl."

Phyl looked shrewd. "Unless the bay casts its spell upon you as it should."

"Spell?"

"When we were children we used to imagine there was a piper on the wind. The name, you know, means songs upon the wind, and one of our stories was about someone who came here to heal a broken heart and found enchantment and never left the bay, marrying the man of her heart."

Chloe said slowly, because she knew she already had had a spell worked upon her, "But wasn't there one who didn't find enchantment here and fled back to England?"

"Yes, but those were tougher, more isolated days and she had a stupid husband who didn't understand how much she missed the greater refinements of the life she had left, although eventually she was prepared to come back with him, but he died before they could. But that's an old story and a sad one — I want your stay here to be all happiness."

Already had she but known it the young woman she was talking to knew that there was only one way it could be all happiness for her. But it seemed as if Merle would be the one to find that fulfilment. She pushed the thought away from her. Just as well, perhaps, that there *was* Merle, for she, Chloe, was just dazzled by this fascination, for her favourite author.

They had a surprise when Saturday's newspaper arrived. It was always left at the big house. Phyl rang, her voice excited, "Do come over, all of you, we've already achieved advance publicity." When they got there, she had it open at the feature page on the kitchen table. Full justice had been done to the project. "There was a woman very keen to take photos but I didn't dream she was a journalist. I put her down as the wife of one of the committee members who was fascinated by the idea."

They read on, Josh and Abbie craning over their shoulders. Phyl watched them a little anxiously as they read the last paragraph. They read it, stared blankly, then at each other and said in a duet, "Where on earth did they get that idea?"

Phyl looked embarrassed. "I'm afraid that

was me. There was an awkward little man there. I rather resented some of the questions he asked and he finished up quite snottily when I proclaimed proudly that we were bringing an interior decorator out from England. It seems he'd already had word of this. His wife is a friend of Beatrice's who had rung Merle last night to see when Beatrice was coming home — wanted to know if she'd speak on Singapore at their wretched club next week — and as Dane had told Merle on the phone what he was doing, Merle told her. This man had said 'My word, we are getting grandiose ideas, aren't we? I've always heard success goes to the head. What's wrong with employing a local firm?' "

Chloe looked unhappy. "I told Dane that could happen but this last sentence I don't understand."

They all studied it again. The report read: 'But evidently romance is not just to be found in the pages of Dane Inglethorpe's thrillers; it seems as if it is in the air, and what more romantic than bringing out the one his fancy has alighted upon, to redecorate the homestead of his ancestors.'

Chloe moaned. But Dane's eyes were on his sister's face. "Come on, Phyl, you're looking guilty. What did you say to give that impression?"

She shifted her gaze away from those knowing tawny eyes. "Well . . . er . . . I didn't want letters to the paper demanding why local labour wasn't being employed, so I . . . er . . . kind of hinted Chloe was being brought out to give the place the once-over and wasn't it a coincidence she happened to be an employee of one of Britain's most famous restorers! That's all!" This last was said with a hint of defiance.

To Chloe's surprise Dane guffawed. "Well, for a spur of the moment fabrication you did very well, Sis. The art of diplomacy must be part of your make-up."

Phyl looked relieved but there was a frown on Chloe's brow. "Oh dear, I do hope this doesn't get taken for gospel by anyone to whom it might matter!"

They gazed at her uncomfortably. "Well, what of it?"

Chloe said, "We'd better be rather distant with each other fairly soon to disabuse anyone moved by such a quaint idea."

Dane enquired, with great would-be seriousness, "It would be interesting to know which you find quaint — that you should fall for me, or that I should fall for you? I'd rather think both ideas are acceptable."

Chloe banged her fist on the table. "Always the gallant answer — the witty dialogue. It's just ridiculous."

He chuckled. "Leave it be. It could be it fits in with some plans I've had ever since we first met. It's the stuff stories are made of."

Chloe sighed. "Oh you're impossible. So it serves you right if the idea backfires on you. *I'll* do nothing to further this fancy."

"But you won't throw a spanner in the works, either, will you?" said Ross anxiously.

Chloe relented. "But don't try me too far. Don't expect me to cast loving glances Dane's way, or foster any other signs of affection."

"Now that," said Dane, "sounds like a dirty slam to me."

"It was meant to," Chloe retorted.

He flung up his hands in mock despair. "First of all she suspects any compliments I pay her, as something insincere — just part of the author syndrome — and now this!"

Chloe said darkly, "You ought to be worried lest it scare off anyone else on the horizon in your love life."

"Stop dissecting me. I feel like an ant under a microscope. And anyway if any of this gets me publicity I'll probably slay my sister. Oh it's okay, Sis, I realise you had to nip any criticism in the bud, but don't get carried away."

Chloe said, "I can see it's very dangerous living with two people with such imaginations."

Abbie had come in and heard most of this. Mischief lit her eyes. "Now if that had happened to me when I was young, I'd have enjoyed every moment of it."

"You're all impossible," declared Chloe.

Chloe loved Christchurch. The cathedral at the heart of the city, with its spire patterned on that of Salisbury Cathedral; its halls of learning, the gentle Avon so different from the turbulent rivers that carried away snow-waters and glacier-melt to the sea; canoes, largely manned by schoolboys in striped blazers, the squares named after British martyrs, the streets that were called after British bishoprics — Worcester, Gloucester, for instance.

Phyl took her into the cathedral to get the feel of it. She stood for a moment, her hand on the effigy of John Chitty Harper, the first bishop of the colony, a wonderful man, not particularly young, who had left a comfortable diocese in the old country to minister to the flock here, and because of the size of some of the unbridged rivers — the Rakaia for instance, a mile and a tenth wide — he sometimes had to take his clothes off and swim his horse over them.

Phyl started to laugh. "Our grandmother told us that when she went to live in mid-Canterbury, she was a little puzzled by the way people were speaking of 'the Bishop' because some of the stories sounded out of date. Then she realised they weren't speaking of the bishop of the day — Bishop Harper was still remembered as *the* Bishop. She found it most endearing. The story she liked best was when a certain spot on a river bank was pointed out to her as 'that's where the Bishop got bucked off his horse'. Thereby hung a tale, because the reverend gentleman was wearing a top hat, landed on his head, and it was pushed down over his nose! His family of beautiful daughters were snapped up by aspiring landowners and even today some of our top ten families are descendants of the Bishop."

"We must get a photo of him somehow and give it a place in some room at least," Chloe suggested.

Phyl hugged her, "You are going to steep us all, family and customers alike, in the vigorous history of the young church colony."

Chloe knew she was becoming almost obsessed with it, something she dared not analyse because she didn't know how much of it was due to a new background, and the beauty of her surroundings, or to the magic of working side by side with Dane. What a compelling mixture of a man: at home in the saddle, riding these tussocky hills, in the woolshed, out in the garden of the first homestead, entering into the children's interests, sitting at night in the small room that once had been the sitting-room of colonial days, or demanding that she come out in the launch with him exploring other small bays and even over to Lyttelton and out to the Heads. When she protested that all this was taking him away from his desk he just laughed.

"It's so important you get the full feel of this venture; it's most necessary for you to impart the flavour of our beginnings to the surroundings where local people and tourists alike will come to admire and wonder — and keep coming. Hauroko Bay was suffering from the down-turn of the overseas markets — and for Ross and Phyl's sakes it's got to be made a viable proposition again. In fact to sing a new song. I like that definition of that name — do you? Songs upon the Wind."

"Oh, I do. People who don't thrill to the

meaning of that have no soul."

He nodded. "Like people who don't get stirred by the sound of trumpets. That's something that really makes the blood leap." His eyes were on her, watching her reaction to that. He got it. Her eyes were a glow.

She turned to him and said, "Yet there are people who *don't* thrill to that. Unimaginative people. I'm so glad I've met an author who does."

They were standing under a pear tree in full bloom; bees were tumbling in and out of their scented depths, a little sea breeze came up to blow the coppery hair back from her brow. He caught her hands, said, "And I'm glad, so glad, you came with me to my home. You're such an inspiration, Chloe." He leaned forward and kissed her, full on the mouth. She uttered, rather breathlessly, "More of the susceptible author touch?" and waited for his answer. It came. A single word . . . "No", and at that moment Sarah and Pip came racing through the orchard, home from school.

Chapter Five

There was little time for moments like that. A small army of workmen descended on the bay, eager for work, most of them extremely keen on the idea. Walls were replastered and repapered, some of them in the style of yesteryear. The golds of early spring gave way to the purples of lilac and wisteria, and the avenue of hawthorns took on rose and cream clusters. Heloise grew long-legged and even more beautiful, day by day. By now Chloe had inspected the first house in that forsaken village street where Joshua and Abbie were to live when Dane married. Merle rode over often, the very epitome of equestrienne grace. Sometimes, fortunately not often, she brought Beatrice over in the car.

She said to Chloe one day when she'd expressed a desire to see the wing that was to be part of the project, "I'm afraid Dad's getting rather tired of Beatrice. He's always having to pour oil on troubled waters with someone or other."

Chloe replied cautiously, "Then why does he put up with her? She's not related to him, is she? Does she not have a home of her own? I'm not sure of the relationship."

"She looks on me as a sort of daughter. She came to housekeep for us when Mother died. Dad felt otherwise I'd have no life of my own. Decent of him but it pitch-forked a mischief-maker into our midst. At first she had ideas about marrying Dad but he soon made it plain to her that it was just not on. I developed a great respect for my father over that. Of course she had the idea that if she succeeded she'd be part of what she probably looked on as the 'landed gentry' — the aristocracy of the first settlers! As if that sort of thing cuts any ice these days! Trouble was, however, that Dad has a heart as soft as butter and didn't fire her, even when I founded the riding school here, and could easily have managed, with extra staff, to run our homestead too. But Dad was adamant about that — said the time might come when I married, and he had no time for parents who were possessive, that while he hoped I'd still be near enough to keep the riding school going, he wasn't going to have his only daughter suffering a divided loyalty!"

Chloe said warmly, "Oh, I'm sure I will love your father. In my work back home I've seen so many of the younger generation tied to crumbling ruins because of tradition and family solidarity; even letting it devastate their own love life."

Merle lifted her chin and said with supreme confidence, "Well it certainly isn't going to devastate mine."

Chloe felt a lurch of the heart, a lowering of her spirits. This was not only a lovely girl, she was so likeable. What had been meant by that? Why, that she and Dane lived in adjoining bays — only a hill between, with common interests, even possibly financial links. How ideal it would seem, especially now, with the influx of people to what was sure to become a great attraction; something that would bring custom also to the riding school, she supposed.

At that moment one of the workmen came in. "I'd like to see you about something, Chloe, if I can break in?"

Merle said immediately, "I must be off. I only rode over to see Heloise. A real little beauty."

The workman looked after her. "Who on earth is Heloise?"

Chloe laughed. "A little filly. Her mother's name is Hildegarde. They let me name the foal."

"Who better!" he commented.

Chloe looked at him closely, "Why?"

He chuckled. "Well, it seemed from that newspaper article, your destiny is here."

She'd noticed before that this man, Barry, had a fine vocabulary. She dared not disclaim this, as she didn't want him dropping any hints to his mates that things were not what they seemed — that she'd been brought here simply and solely for the job. It took so little to stir resentment.

Barry asked now, with a sort of cheerful effrontery, "I reckon Dane must have felt there was a planned pattern in this . . . meeting you, falling for you, the ideal person for this project."

"Indeed, I think so too," said a voice behind them. Dane's. The audacious glint now so familiar to her, was in his eyes. "Things do happen now and then in the true spirit of romance . . . a sort of design for life. I'm a very lucky man."

Oh dear, this was going too far. Did Dane never think how it could affect things between Merle and himself? But perhaps he had already explained it to her and she was going along with it so there'd be no discord or resentment. Chloe felt that for his own sake she must slow him down. With his fertile imagination there was no knowing what he'd say next, so she changed the subject. "Barry has come to consult with me over something. What is it, Barry?"

The man grinned, "Well it would be best talked over with you both — and you may turn the notion down. My idea was that if Chloe liked it she might persuade you to look at it favourably."

Dane said, "Well, what is it? She can persuade me into most things, so fire ahead."

Barry didn't hesitate. "Well, in my dinner hours I've been looking around here. Especially at that village street. The outsides are well-preserved but the interiors leave a lot to be desired. Have you ever thought of letting them out to people?"

"You mean as holiday houses? Yes, often, but we dare not risk turning our bay into a sort of glorified camping ground. It would be like running motels. We'd run up against all sorts of regulations and, frankly, the idea doesn't appeal. We've enough on our plate, already."

Barry said, "I didn't quite mean that. My wife and I plan to take a trip to Britain in a few years' time to visit our two children who are studying over there and seem more than likely to take positions there. Monica's part-time job in Christchurch is about to fold up and she fell in love with this bay and those houses took her fancy. We wondered if there was any chance of us having one of them, leasing our house in Christchurch to someone, and I'll do up the one we're living in, and — as my wife is fully trained in catering and has done a stint as a waitress besides, she would apply to Ross and Phyl for a job at Inglethorpe House, in the new restaurant."

It didn't take Dane long to make up his mind. "You're on, mate. I'll have to consult Ross and Phyl, of course, but it would be hard to think of a better solution in the matter of staff. Let's all go over and look at whichever one takes your fancy — or would you prefer to wait till your wife can get over?"

Barry said diffidently, "This was her idea in the first place. She said if it possibly came off, she'd love the house opposite the one the vicar and his wife have been promised." He glanced at the pair of them and said, "And maybe it won't be long at that before they need it."

Dane nodded sagely, "You're dead right. Not if I can help it. Come on, let's go."

Oh dear again! thought Chloe. Then he must've explained things to Merle or he wouldn't go on like this. On Beatrice's last visit, when she and Chloe had been left alone together for a few minutes, she had said, "It's wonderful to see those two to-gether again. I felt Merle fretted earlier in the year. They were children together, of course, and Dane, with being a few years older, was most protective of Merle."

Chloe had been surprised. She'd thought Beatrice hadn't been at Pukemata Bay, over the hill, as long as that. Beatrice continued, "Wonderful, too, to know Dane is making such a success of his books — all this must be costing a mint of money, and, after all, it will benefit his sister and her husband more than anyone. However, I'm sure Merle will know how to put the brakes on."

Chloe had been surprised at the rage she felt. Even though it had cut at her to realise how sure Beatrice was that things were go-ing that way, was Dane the type to be domi-nated by a wife to have his generous impulses curtailed?

She let these thoughts recede as they went out of the house, through the apple blossom of the orchard, across the stone humpy-backed bridge, built early in the century by a skilled tradesman old Aubrey had brought out, and up the incline to where the two rows of houses began. The one Barry indi-cated was almost the twin of Joshua and Abbie's, except it lacked a small conserva-tory theirs had on one side. It was very shabby inside, and smelt musty. The walls had been white washed so long ago they were peeling and from old-fashioned picture rails you could see tell tale signs where pictures had been hung. But Barry seemed even enchanted with it.

"Tell me, did my sister meet your wife when she was over here? I mean, did they appear to click?" Dane asked him.

"Yes, that was what started it all. Monica coveted a job here and loved the bay. Phyl spent longer with her than with the others because from one or two remarks Monica made, Phyl seemed interested as one caterer to another."

"Good. Because the distance around the harbour here won't make it easy to get full or half-time workers. Let's go over and see my sister now."

"Well, you won't need me," said Chloe, preparing to depart. "I'll go over to Josh and Abbie's choice while I'm here and do some rough sketches for them. I know it will be long enough before their house is needed, but, just as you like to brood upon your stories, Dane, for a long time before you set pen to paper — or do I mean key the word processor? — so I like to dream over any project till I get the right gut feeling about it."

"Fair enough but I want you with us just the same." Again the glint in the eye, "Because who knows — we might need their house quite soon."

"And I'm with you in wishing that," endorsed Barry, "if I was in your shoes I wouldn't want to wait longer than I had to." His eyes looked appreciatively at this coppery-headed girl, in faded jeans, hair hanging down her back in a russet-coloured plait.

"Oh, you're someone after my own heart." Dane put an arm round Chloe's shoulders and they moved out into the radiance of a late September day in the southern hemisphere. Chloe contented herself with one glare at him as they stepped out behind Barry.

Phyl was thrilled. That would be one less worry for her. Someone she'd already taken a fancy to, able to work a double role in preparing meals, and perhaps serving them, was in the nature of a godsend. They arranged for Monica to come over at the weekend. As they were leaving Barry added, "She was a farmer's daughter before she married me. So in an emergency she can lamb a ewe with the best of them!"

"The right qualifications for here," declared Dane.

They lingered for some time over the

house opposite Josh and Abbie's. It was delightful, with a narrow stairway that led up to dormer-windowed bedrooms. Not convenient by modern standards but that didn't present much of an obstacle, and windows could be enlarged or extra ones put in to give more light. Chloe jotted down a few ideas there and then and drew some rough sketches she could work on tonight but warned them Monica might have some cherished ideas of her own. Then Barry went back to his own work and Chloe and Dane were left looking at each other.

He said with determination, "I don't feel like settling down in the study again. I think we ought to be celebrating — but with a crowd like this hammering and sawing and plastering, it's not possible." He smiled at her. "Come on girl, down to the shore with me. The tide is coming in." He grasped her hand and they went running down. Chloe caught his mood and stopped thinking about Merle.

They had the bay to themselves. She fished in the pockets of those faded jeans and brought out a shoelace. Dane looked startled. "What on earth's that for? What an urchin you look. Like some schoolboy with a conglomeration of bits and pieces in his pockets."

Her plait had lost the ribbon that had fastened it as they ran. With a gesture of impatience she shook it free and tied her hair back, hair that had a curious quality of its own, an exuberance of coppery tresses. "I can't stand my hair blowing into my eyes when I'm by the sea. It's distracting. That water looks tempting — I know it's still quite cold, but here goes." She kicked off her thonged sandals, rolled up the ancient jeans, then said, "Oh, how I love the flotsam that comes ashore here. No wonder Pip loves it. Her mother tells me that's why she makes deep pockets in those rather long skirts that child wears. Oh — look — there's a dead starfish. I wonder what tales it could tell." She put it in her pocket. "See, the tide's filling those pools in the rocks — I must see them. Just the place for sea anemones." She plunged in, wading, and hadn't doubled the jeans up far enough so was soaked in a moment.

Dane was in shorts so he kicked off his footwear and plunged in after her. "You are far too venturesome — tides change and the pools that were shallow yesterday could be deeper today in this strengthening wind."

She laughed and waited for him to catch her up, the breeze outlining her top. He

120

caught up with her and held her in a grip that would keep her from going further and guided her along the far rocks where the sand sloped upwards. "Plenty of pools here to satisfy you, madcap."

She stood still, caught in the spell of his masculine strength. No desk-wallah this; a man with a vivid imagination, yet he belonged to the great open spaces, the tussocky hills, the sea.

He looked down on her, that smile grooving the lines about his mouth, and said, "You are quite enchanting, you know." He bent his head and brought his mouth down on hers, a very different kiss from the goodnight one he'd given her on the plane. She was startled and quite incapable of resisting him. The wash of the encroaching waters pushed them a little closer.

She felt breathless, unsure of herself, but said lightly, "I didn't realise kissing was part of the celebration."

He still had a firm hold of her. She was tall too, but had to look up at him. "It wasn't intended to be part of the celebration," he breathed, "but that was an irresistible impulse so don't downgrade it."

She said, looking seriously into his eyes, "I think you're on a high. Things are going well with your book, I dare say, and Barry and his Monica wanting to come here put you in this mood."

He laughed. "No, that wasn't it and you're purposely putting it into a mood of the moment."

She said, still striving for lightness, "Well, what else? You know that repeat we saw on TV last night — the signature tune. Rather catchy. It says: 'a kiss is just a kiss, a sigh is just a sigh'. That's the correct category. Now come on, I want to see what's in those pools. They're filling up."

He still held her, reluctant to open his arms. "You are wrong you know — that wasn't just a kiss, it was a commitment."

She didn't know how to respond to that. She turned her head away and looked down into the nearest pool, and then her attention was caught. "Oh look . . . something I've always wanted to see . . . a live sea horse. What a magic moment."

He bent down, scooped it up. It turned its shapely head and regarded him with bright eyes that flashed in the sunlight. She put out a finger and stroked it as it lay in the hands full of sea water. Then he put it down and it disappeared in the emerald green bubbles. All her embarrassment had fled. "I've always wanted just that. Sheer magic."

He moved her away from the rocks, on to higher sand where just little frills of water, edged with foam, washed gently over their feet and ebbed away again.

He said deliberately, "Yes, there is sheer magic abroad today."

She pronounced quickly, "It so reminded one of a poem my great-grandmother wrote. Leonora treasured her scrapbook and gave it to me when I was about twelve and just waking to the appreciation of Shakespeare and Walter de la Mare and a host of others. But because this was more intimate — I remembered Greeny quite distinctly even though I was so small when she died — it meant a lot to me."

"Greeny? Don't you mean Granny? But perhaps they couldn't expect a child to say 'Great-Granny'."

"No, it was a combination of Granny and what Big Grandad called her. He always called her Renie. As I grew older I appreciated the poem even more."

"I'd like to read it," he told her sincerely. "You won't have a copy with you of course?"

She looked full at him. "I know it by heart. I used to do recitations at school concerts and this fitted the theme of a play we put on once — about life not being dull and prosaic, but holding something of wonder and beauty. I'll write it down for you sometime if you like because it fits this setting."

"If you know it by heart you'll say it for me here and now. There might never be another moment quite like this." His eyes stared into hers. "I'm waiting for you to start, Chloe."

She looked away a little from that searching gaze and began.

" 'Can I describe magic? No, not I . . .
It's the touch of baby fingers or a sunset
   sky;
Sometimes it's sheer enchantment when
   memories come to bless,
Sometimes remembered kisses that drive
   out loneliness . . .
And banish guilt . . . so do not close your
   heart
To any solace; let the magic start
To heal the loss, the rue, the bitter
   pain
And let this world's strange magic loose
   again.
So what is magic? Sun and moon and
   wind,
The glimpse of hills when morning mists
   have thinned . . .

The tranquil waters where the tall ships
  ride,
The treasures that were mine with every
  tide,
Sea horses, starfish, oyster shells and
  more,
Washed to my feet upon that far-flung
  shore . . .
Magic? Go find it lest it pass you by,
The sun, the sea, the moon, the starlit
  sky.' "

There was quite a silence. Then Dane said, a slight tremor in his voice that showed how moved he was, "Thank you, Chloe, that was perfect for today. It could have been written for here. What a gem. I wonder if I might be allowed to use it in the dedication of my current book? I'll write to Leonora and find out if there's a copyright."

"It was never published, but she wrote it in her scrapbook. It's so long ago."

They picked up their footwear, dried their feet with a handkerchief Dane pulled from his pocket and donned their sandals again — because there were thistles on the track that led down to the beach — and went contentedly home.

Ross took on a couple of extra men who

came from Governor's Bay each day. "I don't want Dane to get drawn into the farm work too much. He's not spending enough time at his desk, and after all," he grinned, "that's what's making all this possible."

So there were hours when Dane shut himself away, with his word processor and his muse, and other times when she would sense he wasn't really with them. Abbie laughed about it to Chloe. "Never feel offended if he looks at you as if you were a landscape, or is terse and monosyllabic. His hero and heroine are probably at odds with each other. Don't ever think it's in any way your fault."

Chloe said seriously, "Does he get that way with Merle?"

Abbie shook her head. "No, I don't think he ever has. But then they've known each other so long and understand each other." It sounded special, as it was, of course.

Phyl and Chloe had many trips to the city choosing furnishing materials, visiting picture framers, hunting around second-hand shops for early colonial china and ornaments. Dane shut himself up in his study when they would take off, and, apart from the hours at his desk, seemed to have a lot of business to be conducted by phone to London or via his fax machine.

He emerged from a long spell of this to be surprised at how much they had accomplished. The restaurant was nearly finished. Then Chloe consulted him and Phyl about the little rooms that led off it on two sides, as distinct from the others that housed the kitchen and the serving area. "You've got the air of one dying to spring something on us." Very astute of them.

She sounded apologetic. "You may think it's just the antique shop strain cropping up in me, but I'd love to devote these rooms to special events connected with the early history of the harbour."

"Such as?" they demanded.

"Well, we've got enough historic value pictures between the windows in the restaurant to whet their appetite for more knowledge. Sets of pictures here might even stir up memories of other early ones stashed away in some lumber room, and I've no doubt we could get permission to use others from the excellent books that have been published through the years."

Dane said, "And I guess you already know who to apply to judging by the devoted reading you do night after night." He turned to his sister. "Despite me indicating on my shelves some of my earlier works, articles and so on, she's lost all interest in *my* writing." There was a teasing note in his voice.

Chloe made an impatient gesture. "You know perfectly well that it's because I'm here for so short a time, I have to get on with the job in hand. It's what it's all about."

Phyl said, "I keep forgetting you're not permanently involved with us, with New Zealand. I can't think of you as not being here to see it becoming a success, of supervising house after house of the village street. I've got so many ideas about that — some of them too grandiose I suppose. But I keep seeing this as a community such as it used to be, all working for the common good."

Chloe waited for Dane to say something. But he didn't. Well, it had been said that sometimes silence can be eloquent. Perhaps he thought those ideas *were* too grandiose. Or what?

Phyl continued, "Dane, I think she should meet our grandmother. What she has experienced in her long life and her wonderful memory, would enhance it all, I'm sure. Especially if one room is to be dedicated to Captain Scott's memorabilia, I suppose."

He said quietly, "I intend taking her to meet Gran and Grandad this week in any case, though not for the same reason." Phyl looked at him sharply. He didn't elaborate. He turned to Chloe. "It's not far — about an hour's run from Christchurch and Phyl's idea has its points. There is a strong personal link there with Scott."

"How could there be? Even at your grandmother's age, and I suppose she's in her eighties, it's hardly likely."

"She's well on in her eighties of course, seeing she's Joshua's mother — but then she married at nineteen — and though he's retired, that only came about because he developed a dodgy heart complaint. But it's more a question of who she knew. Gran had — has — a great gift for friendship as well as a knack for putting words together. She has more than one article that will interest you, published by the newspapers of the day."

"Oh, then that's where you get your talent from."

"It's thought so. Right, say Thursday."

She already loved Christchurch, the Garden City as it was called . . . the green-banked Avon flowing sweetly through; its beautiful bridges, the weeping willows that drooped so gracefully above their reflections; willows that, as in Akaroa, had been brought as cuttings, long ago, from Napoleon's tomb on its lonely island. To satisfy a whim of his, Dane took her over the Worcester Street bridge, an ornament in itself in its fine artistry, so she could see where Robert Falcon Scott's magnificent statue stood, lovingly sculpted years ago by his wife.

Dane raised a hand in salute as they passed, and remarked, "Hard to believe now what a courageous thing that was, then, with now planes taking off from this very airport so frequently. It's a whole new world."

They headed for the Great South Road. "I believe those roses are in bud — could they be?" asked Chloe.

"Yes, so they are. It's an early season. Perhaps put on specially for you — and you deserve it."

Always the gallant compliment. Did words come too easily to him? She took herself to task . . . hadn't she despised the boring Hudson because he was so unromantic? And she so wanted this man to be sincere.

Dane didn't know her mood. "Gran says that when Christchurch wasn't so affluent, in the great Depression for instance, and they had mainly grey, splintering paling fences dividing the quarter-acre sections from each other, there was nothing prettier than red roses nodding against the grey. Imagine it: rough, homely and exquisite."

Chloe said, "I love the many mown strips and flower plots outside the fences, and these trees look as if they've been here for centuries."

"It's because the soil was so fertile, which reminds me that when I was touring in Austria the courier pointed out some rather nondescript pines and said it had been one of the Empress Maria Theresa's schemes for redeeming the land from swamp. I thought he was way off beam, the trees were so small and said so to the guy next to me who was a New Zealander and he replied, 'He's dead right. They had a poor start to begin with and nothing like the pace of ours.' No wonder the pioneers thought this was a land flowing with milk and honey. It's very hard to have a true perspective on things when you switch from one hemisphere to another."

He waited for a comment, then, "Do you feel like that, Chloe? I know you love the beauty and the freedom, the great open spaces, if you like, but despite the zest you bring to your job, does it sometimes make you feel strange? Unreal?"

She took a few moments to consider that. "Not as strange as I thought I would. Perhaps due to the welcome I got from everyone. Well, almost everyone." She thought Beatrice had scarcely been cordial. But perhaps she felt Chloe constituted a threat to the girl she looked upon as a daughter? Guilt touched Chloe's consciousness fleetingly. She shook it off. She would enjoy today and remember it when, before long, she was at the other side of the world.

Then they were over the Rakaia River. The spelling amused her. "I'd imagined it spelt Rukya. What does it mean?"

"Um . . . it really means adorned but is probably the South Island form of *rangaia* meaning ranks, which refers to the need for strong men to stand in ranks to break the force of the current for the weaker ones when attempting to ford the river; breaking the current you see. That sensible custom is often used by adventurous tramping parties in similar circumstances."

She shivered as she looked at it; over a mile wide, intersected by great banks of shingle formed into islands where quite tall bushes of colourful lupins and even young willows grew. "And to think of the Bishop facing this sort of thing — and you said he wasn't a young man."

"No — later one of his daughters got swept downstream when she was crossing it with her husband. The distraught man was running along the bank calling, 'I'll see you in heaven, dear', which was probably of little comfort to her then, but she was swept onto one of the islands and, in the end, was little the worse for her adventure."

They turned westward facing the mountains still glistening from their winter snows and could see the narrow cliff where the Rakaia forced through. "Grandad's run is on this bank; one of their sons, my uncle Randolph, manages it now. Gran and Grandad built a smaller place on the property. It's quite secluded. He built great shelter breaks around his precious garden to shield it from the nor'westers. This area is called the dust bowl of the Pacific; there's a property at the head of the gorge called Windwhistle — the only name for it."

So she came to 'Wheatacres' armed with knowledge. Hard to believe Lucy Winchmore was in her eighties. She had an eagerness, a zest for life just as Dane had described her. She had a midday dinner ready for them, roast hogget, peas, *kumera*, the native sweet potato Chloe was already addicted to, potatoes cooked round the meat, mint sauce and red currant jelly for those who fancied it, and an apple sponge with cream to follow.

Dane greeted her. "How goes it, Gran? As I told you on the phone I want you to talk about your friendship, so long ago, with Anne Hardy."

"I could just give her the article," his grandmother said.

He shook his head. "No, in your own words and in your inimitable style. You'll make it live that way."

She began, and as she spoke of the 'Grand Old Lady of Rakaia' her eyes kindled and Chloe listened, fascinated. "We came here when I was forty-two, after we sold our run in North Canterbury and, as a newcomer, I was taken to see the Grand Old Lady who was eighty-four, twice my age. We took an instant liking for each other. Think on that, my dear — when you're forty-two there may be a baby born, whom you'll recognise for a kindred spirit when you meet her at eighty-four.

"She lived in a small unit and was most contented to be there, surrounded by her treasures, and they *were* treasures, believe me. Her father was a Member of Parliament and because there was a large family, and quite a young one, Anne was the one who accompanied him to Wellington when the house was sitting, and acted as his hostess. Because of this she met all the prominent people of the day and garnered experiences that were to enrich her whole life. She lent me her scrapbook that was also kept as a journal and I found a page on which she had written 'My memory-box is being rapidly filled with stores to last me the rest of my life!' It made me, too, Chloe, recognise the worth of some experiences that happened to me — good and bad.

"Those memories of hers looked back to the more leisurely existence of last century recalling pioneer names, the social life in the country, the tennis parties at Rokeby, the estate where the Lyttelton family lived, when they played in ankle-length white dresses with hems heavily braided to save them from the occasional encounter with dirt.

"She was a great friend of Edith Lyttelton of Rokeby who later was revealed as the author, a controversial one, who wrote under the name G.B. Lancaster. The Lyttelton family went back to England and of course our governor general of a few years ago belonged to it, Lord Cobham. But I digress.

"Anne met Edward Wilson who accompanied Scott to the Antarctic and perished with him, and she and his wife, a bride of just three weeks when her husband left on the first expedition, became fast friends.

"At a tea party prior to the last venture, Edward told Miss Hardy that if she liked to give him a silk Union Jack no larger than a lady's handkerchief he would take it to the South Pole for her and hope to bring it back.

"Mrs Wilson was in New Zealand to greet their return, was to have spent the night with Anne but for some reason went further south and was on the northbound train when the paper boys came through the train, crying out news of the tragedy. And there it was, on her wall, framed, the red, white and blue of the little flag that had been found on his body. Mrs Wilson had returned it to Anne on the Monday or Tuesday of the following week and in the accompanying note said she had just attended Divine Service at Sumner and had been so close in spirit to her gallant husband. She wrote, simply, 'I have been to Church with Ted!'

"I touched the frame reverently. It was side-by-side with an autographed photograph of Scott himself."

Chloe wiped her tears away. Lucy Winchmore smiled gently. "Thank you my dear, I appreciate you shedding tears for a tragedy of yesteryear." Then with a change of tone she said briskly, "And now you'll want to be on your way. Thank you for bringing her to me, Dane. I approve in every way. Are you going straight home?"

He shook his head and grinned. "No, I'm giving Chloe tea at the Sign of the Kiwi.

There was quite an atmosphere at breakfast this morning, chilly. Joshua and Abbie had had one of their rare spats. I heard them as I went to the shower. Josh said in that no-nonsense tone he uses so seldom, 'No, Abbie, I absolutely forbid you to mention the subject to either of them. You're getting carried away by the thought we could be in a place of our own sooner than hoped for.' "

Lucy chuckled, "And he so rarely puts his foot down, dear Abbie would submit. I know my eldest son so well. But she would be frosty, to show him she wasn't entirely subdued. Good for her." It must've reminded her of something. "And Dane, dear boy, be kind to Merle just now. Her feelings are fragile at the moment. She came to see me last week. I didn't know what to make of it. So — it's over to you."

Chloe had loved Lucy from the moment they met, but now she was aware of an instant chill. She mustn't let her feelings show. She didn't want to be remembered as someone who'd caused a crack in the lute. Didn't they, couldn't they realise it was the ebullient spirit of an author making him appear to be paying particular interest to the stranger in their midst? But, of course, they had known him since childhood and perhaps didn't recognise it for what it was.

She felt she'd rather have been going home for the evening meal. Every moment she spent alone with Dane she was in danger of revealing her feelings. She was afraid of the unguarded moment, afraid of the sound of her own voice as she answered him, finding in him all she'd ever hoped for in a man . . . the matching thought, the same delight in this lovely world, the sense of fun, the male attractiveness . . . yes, all she'd ever hoped to meet . . . a true blend of the physical, the spirit, the comradeship.

Dane said softly "Tired? You're very quiet." His hand came across to one of hers as it lay on her lap. "Perhaps you're a little bit homesick. I'm in danger of forgetting this is all alien to you. Not your natural sphere."

Alien? Not her natural sphere? What was that saying? Home is where the heart is!

"I'm not homesick, Dane, it's just that my mind is too full of all that's been told me today. I've been back in another age . . . in a world before the Great War as they used to call it, long before the Second World War. In another era where ankle-length skirts were seen on tennis courts, where the South Pole was still an unknown continent in the main . . . and now men and women even winter down there, and a long-ago tragedy becomes something today that seems as if it has just happened yesterday, because we live on that glorious harbour whence the *Terra Nova* sailed all those years ago."

There was a smile in his voice. "You'd be invaluable as a secretary to a writer, Chloe. Not just an inspiration, but a practical help too. Fancy the role?"

She made her tone purposely casual. "No, not particularly. My line is more in the nature of interior decorating, remember?"

"Well, you're in the right place, aren't you? That row of derelict houses could keep you going for years. To say nothing of the old homestead. Ever thought you'd like the chance of doing that up? Any ideas about it?"

She forgot to be casual. "Any ideas? It's taken my fancy more than anything. I can see it as it was once, with dim shadowy drapes and old Axminster carpets, all in pastel shades. That little bedroom off Josh and Abbie's fascinates me. She says it belongs to the days when there was always a current baby, and that babies must have lain awake watching the shadows of that old cherry tree on the ceiling, to say nothing of the way the light changes there, as the sun goes behind some hill or emerges from others. The effect is almost like a prism. That's an idea — the drawing-room faces the same way, you ought to get one or two prisms for it. Perhaps in some second-hand shop. We had a lovely set back home. I mean in the showroom."

He suggested, "Perhaps we could get Leonora to pay us a visit and bring it out with her."

"Idiot," she said, carefully surpressing the instant wish that that might be possible.

"I don't see why not. She was the one who triggered all this off. She'd known the bay for so long, from those sketches."

"Not just the bay," she reminded him, "but the Kaikoura coast too, and even one of Wellington Harbour. The artist must have moved around a fair bit for those days." They were in Christchurch traffic now.

Eventually they drove up the lonelier road to the Sign of the Kiwi and as they did, welcoming lights switched on. Dusk was holding these hills and the city below in purple shadows.

"I believe there'll be a moon tonight," Dane said. "It would be a new experience for you to see it over the plains instead of making a moon-track across the harbour waters."

She turned to him. "Use that in a book some time."

He sighed. "You see everything in terms of books as far as I'm concerned. Are you obsessed with me being an author and don't see me as a man at all? I sometimes wish I could shake off the image."

Oh no. She was far too aware of him as a man. *That* she knew. "You also talk a lot of nonsense, Dane," she told him severely.

She was enchanted with the Kiwi from the moment they went under the beam of the entrance porch where, carved into it was the text: 'Jog on, jog on, the footpath way, and merrily hent the stile-a, a merry heart goes all the way, your sad tires in a mile-a.'

"Where is that from, Dane? It's Shakespeare, isn't it?"

"Yes — from *The Winter's Tale*. I looked it up once."

"I so like to know these sources, and to picture where they were written as well as by whom. I can see the surroundings and the difficulties they laboured under. No typewriters, no wordprocessors, sometimes even candles failed them and some lines must have been written by rush light, reeking the air and probably throwing shadows all the wrong way. How could the immortal bard dream his words would echo for centuries and even adorn a country like this, undiscovered then by the other hemisphere?"

It stopped Dane dead. he looked down into her face, said unevenly, "I don't think you have any idea what an inspiration you are."

She caught in her breath. That was something she would remember and treasure always.

He swung round and looked down at the darkening scene below and said oddly, "Isn't it strange? Now Merle would only see moths flying against the light, or listen for the night birds calling. She can identify every one, though. She and Pip are a pair in that, just as she and Sarah are over the horses."

Chloe reflected on that. What did it matter? Just that they met on different levels, but because Dane's business was with words, in this, at least she and Dane were closer.

As soon as they entered the inner room, they were accorded quite a welcome and told they'd kept the special table for them.

"Why special, Dane?"

"Because this was the one my grandmother and her mother always sat at. Wonderful for her when this place was restored again. During the war it fell into disrepair and vandals broke in. It had always been run, lonely and all as it was, by the wife of the caretaker of the time, but then most able-bodied men were away in the various theatres of war. When Gran came here first it was magnificent. The china was especially made for them by Royal Doulton — the plates had a design of kiwis marching all around the rims — and teapot, sugar basin and milk jug were of that blue speckled Moorcroft ware. Josh and Uncle Randolph bought their mother and father a set, plus a teapot stand with a silver rim, for their silver wedding and now Gran wishes it hadn't been used every day — the teapot was smashed, and they now fetch seven hundred dollars! There is some on show in that glass case over there; even some fragments dug up when they were excavating for some extensions."

The table was in the corner between the stone fireplace and the window that looked down the winding road where cars with purring engines and amber eyes like cats, were coming uphill. Some parked and came in, some went on to Governor's Bay or Lyttelton, perhaps to over-harbour bays.

Dane, biting into crisp freshly-baked

scones topped with raspberry jam and cream, said, "You asked was the word 'hent' ever used these days, but then the waitress arrived. No, I looked it up once. Gran had said to the curious little boy I was: 'Look it up. That's what dictionaries are for and the sooner you get into the habit of using them, the faster you'll educate yourself.' It's archaic, meant originally to grasp, to take, to snatch or carry off. There are two references to Shakespeare in the definition, one is to reach."

"I like it. I think stiles are romantic. There's something about mounting them. There were quite a few in the valley of the Tyne we loved so much in our childhood, and of course, some along those lovely public paths all over England. They keep that rural touch, I hope they never disappear. They've a touch of magic about them."

"Like that poem you quoted to me, down at the shore. Another link between hemispheres, that these things exist in both places."

"Yes, like the crocuses. Phyl took me to see them along the banks of the Millbrook Reserve, when I first went with her to Christchurch to interview firms re certain patterns of fabrics. There were bluebells too and she said sometimes there's a day set aside for bulb planting. By jove, Dane, these are good. When I was eating Lucy's roast lamb I couldn't imagine being hungry again today, but I am."

What a contrast this provided, talking of stiles and looking out at the enormous building of the TV transmitter on Sugar Loaf. She commented on it.

"Yes, but there are still paddocks close to it, and sheep baaing. The old and the new closely wedded."

They lingered while he told her the story of Harry Ell whose dream it was, long ago, to build a chain of roadhouses across the Port Hills to tempt the youth and the not-so-young of the city to forsake the plains in their leisure time and climb these heights. "A poetic thought, Chloe, because when you climb a hill, or a mountain, you set the horizon further away and widen your own understanding."

She thought she'd better not say: "Use that in a book sometime." Remarks like that seemed to rile him. A pity, in any case, to stop him in mid-flow.

"He was a man of unbelievable variety and tenaciousness. How he crammed so much into one lifetime we'll never know. He has been described as a turbulent spirit or a thorn in the side of the council of the day, but although the completion of the Summit Road is what he is chiefly remembered for, he had a distinguished parliamentary career for a score of years, did a lot to improve conditions in mental hospitals, tuberculosis sanitoriums — that scourge of the past — to say nothing of the preservation of the native bush and bird life of New Zealand. He's one of Merle's great heroes. Sometimes I wish he could have known of the walking tracks and farm overnight stops that now exist from Akaroa, the other harbour on the far side.

"The story I like best about Harry Ell and which proves this man's greatness, is closely related to our family, because Gran and some fellow companions once came across him kneeling in the dust of an unimportant side track near Victoria Park. He was fitting some flat stones of the hillside into a steep part of this single-file trail in the tussock, to make it easier for older hikers.

"Then years and years later, Lindsey Sigglekow, the wife of the ranger of recent times, dreamed of restoring it to this again, and succeeded beyond her wildest dreams."

Chloe looked directly into his eyes across the table. "Just think — you thought I might find the history of what was then a remote colony, rather raw and uninteresting, but now I'm identifying with it and seeing behind the basic beauty of this place, the dreams and aspirations of what was then, surely, a new world. I've got to make Inglethorpe House worthy of its past."

Chapter Six

They came out feeling in perfect accord with
each other to a scene even more beautiful
than the twilight. In this instance it was a
case of man enhancing nature . . . below
them the wide spreading city had sequinned
the darkness with a myriad lights from the
clearly defined rows of lampposts, to floodlit
landmarks and flashing neon signs.

She stood quite still, entranced with it.
He didn't point out any features to her, let
her find them herself. She turned a little to
the right, and in the light of the rising moon,
she could distinctly distinguish the gleam of
white surf along the almost limitless shore-
line of Pegasus Bay, dotted with the minor
lighting of numerous small townships till it
reached the Kaikoura mountains where, the
divers said, those ravines and peaks continued under the sea. Great whales would be
there, providing amusement in the daylight
for sightseers from all over the world.

She dragged her gaze down from that,
westward, where eternal snows glinted, and
here and there, by the light of the heavens,

were streaks of silver where the mighty rivers plunged through. They shared it in silence, then he took her arm. "I've something else to show you."

She said, surprised, "We left the car on the other side."

"Yes, Chloe, but this first. We said stiles still existed. I know of one here. Thank goodness you didn't wear high heels." He led her away from the area; they mounted a rough edge of clay with rocks embedded and reached a barbed-wire fence, and sure enough, a stile, with beyond it tussock blown silver in the breeze, and almost immediately they were in another world.

"Shakespeare knew a thing or two," he exulted. "He put it into my mind as we ate. Now let me go first so I make sure the ground is even below the other side. I've known puddles scour it out here." At the top of the stile he reached a hand down to her. She came up easily enough. Then he descended and held out both hands. She stepped down to perfectly level ground but he didn't relinquish the hands. He took her in his arms. The crowds at the Sign of the Kiwi might have been miles away. Just themselves, the shadowy outline of the hills, the unmistakable tang of the New Zealand bush rising up to them from the gully below, the tinkle of the tiny stream as it cascaded from rock to rock between the ferns, then she was folded close and very thoroughly kissed.

She didn't stir, caught spellbound. Then slowly, still holding her, he allowed her to regain her breath. He said whimsically, "I hope William Shakespeare found as secluded a stile. He deserved it. And as sweet a companion."

She recovered her composure, muttering, "You know very well he was talking of jogging on, of finishing an uphill journey."

There was laughter in his voice, "Well, I've found the going uphill with you. Now if you dare to utter one word about good copy and all grist to the mill, I'll probably choke you. This moment is ours alone. Not to be analysed. Do you hear me? Incidentally, you know Miles Burford wanted me to have a stronger love interest in my next book? He said, 'You'll get it if you try hard enough' and do you know, it's not been hard at all. I know *you* don't believe in love at first sight but that happens in this book and I'm vain enough to think it will get you — the way it comes about."

Even in the shadow of the hill towards the moonrise he could see her astonishment. "When have I ever said that to you?"

"Well you would have if the subject had ever come up," he asserted brazenly.

"You are quite, quite mad," she declared.

Dane was congratulating himself on a lucky escape. He didn't want her to know he'd been an eavesdropper before meeting her.

"Now, Chloe, look up at the Milky Way. I wonder how many stars it has? Thank goodness there's still something to wonder at. The day all is known will make the world an arid place. Ever seen a rainbow at night? You can't believe your own eyes. I did once, down Southland. That's a great place for rainbows by day."

They saw with delight a falling star, then Chloe said, "I believe you're delaying going home purposely, hoping all will be well between Joshua and Abbie; hoping they'll be in bed."

"Oh, it won't have lasted this long. It never does. Thinking over what I heard I strongly suspect Abbie's been at her old tricks."

"Such as?"

"Matchmaking. Joshua once said she had one fault as a vicar's wife, and that was it. He used to say that no matter how often she came a cropper, she never learned. I believe once she decided to bring two people together working on that old maxim you can find in ancient autograph books: 'He was warned against the woman, she was warned against the man, and if that won't make a marriage, then there's nothing else that can.' When the pair suddenly announced their betrothal — they'd had reasons of their own for keeping the attraction quiet — they told Joshua the only fly in the ointment was that Mrs Winchmore, his wife, didn't like either of them!"

Chloe chuckled, then said, "But I'm glad she has some faults — otherwise she'd be too perfect."

"Well it's a case similar to yours — saying quite suddenly and without second thought whatever has flashed into her mind."

She decided she must be well on the way to overcoming *that* fault. She had suddenly been visited by the unwelcome suspicion that Abbie was probably envisioning a match between Dane and Merle. It would be so ideal. She shut her mind to it.

As they approached the old homestead they saw the house was in darkness save for one upstairs light, Joshua and Abbie's, and as they entered they heard a peal of feminine laughter. If anyone had heard Abbie laugh without actually seeing her, they would have imagined her thirty years younger. It had that quality, irresistible. They heard Joshua's deep chuckle in response. "I must put my foot down more often if it makes you like this. Now, let's finish this crossword. My mother must've kept them late."

Abbie had left them some chicken sandwiches, not forgetting a spread of stuffing, and a thermos jug of coffee. Chloe got up before Dane had quite finished his. "I'm for another shower, Dane. It's been a long day. Thank you for taking me to meet your grandmother. It has enriched me. I read once, I don't know where, that such things arc riches of the mind and treasures of the heart. So was my day."

He said without the ghost of a smile, "You read it in a book by Dane Inglethorpe. A nice compliment. Goodnight, Chloe."

November was the time of roses. They festooned every trellis, every arch. Some were old-fashioned cottage roses grown, she learned with delight, from cuttings of the first bushes brought out on sailing ships, wrapped in sacking and kept moist with every rainfall. Chloe loved the clustered creamy ones they called Seven Sisters. Monica Jameson, who was at the bay almost as often as her husband, suggested they had name pegs made for them. "People will wander about these beds and will want to know the names. I've a feeling someone will apply for a gardening position, asking for one of the houses. How do you think Phyl and Ross would react, Chloe?"

"They'd leap at the chance I should think. They can't expect to do it all themselves now, and what a boon to always have fresh flowers for the tables." Chloe paused, then asked, "If we open on New Year's Day what flowers will be in bloom for the next few weeks? I'm all mixed up as regards the seasons. Though I'm getting used to the sun going to the north instead of to the south."

Monica thought. "Lilies and carnations, London Pride, dianthus, larkspur and delphiniums if they're not over. Some early Michaelmas daisies, felicia — do you know it? Lilac-coloured daisies on a little bush, wallflowers, and always geraniums. Oh, we won't be short of flowers, ever, and in this sheltered inlet even winter provides a lot of colour."

Chloe gave a satisfied sigh, then remembered she wouldn't see it in winter.

One morning Dane appeared at the little room under the tower that Chloe used for sketching in. It had been a lumber room for years and she'd done nothing to it save clear a space for an ancient, but sturdy table and chair. She hadn't even put a curtain at the window set in slantingly, that she said was as good as a skylight. She wasn't exactly immersed in interior work: she had sketched out a study of Sarah and Pip running side by side with the foal. She had a yen to give it to Phyl and Ross for Christmas, that strange Christmas in summer that would be so near the grand opening. A family celebration uncluttered by the general public. Phyl had decreed that for her children.

"Is it okay to interrupt?" Dane had a great admiration for the way Chloe respected his need for solitude in his study or when he roamed outside alone, thinking out some sticky problem in his plot.

She lifted her head and nodded. "Look. It's for Ross and Phyl."

"Why, that's enchanting. They'll love it. Well, seeing I won't be holding up any of the workmen depending on your ideas, would you come across to the other bay with me? I want to see Merle rather specially."

"Then you won't want me with you."

"But I do. You know Gran asked me to be kind to her? Jack, her father, rang me last night. Said he knows that deep down something is bothering her but she won't say what. He thought Beatrice might have upset her — sowed some doubt in her mind. He particularly asked me to bring you, said running a riding school means she doesn't have close friends of her own age. Seems to think she's taken a great fancy to you. He'd like to see us first. He'll probably be in the woolshed — nice and private — but in case he's not — because he's got a lamb buyer due sometime this week — then to go up to the house."

Chloe had grave misgivings. Both men were as blind as bats. Couldn't they see *she* could be the bone of contention; that Merle could have doubts of her because Dane was paying her, Chloe, marked attention? But Dane wouldn't take no for an answer. Well, on his own head be it! She'd do some straight talking. Perhaps he too, like his grandmother, didn't *want* to recognise *what* was eating at Merle.

Except for her thoughts Chloe would have enjoyed the drive, a steep one and rough. It wasn't a public road that led from Headland House to Pukemata Bay. There was another road, the public one, that skirted the indented coastline and went on, well past Purau and Diamond Harbour. It was a glorious morning — surely the waters of Diamond Harbour couldn't sparkle more than this. It was so beautiful it almost hurt, perhaps because on the return journey she might not be able to rejoice in it. And Dane himself would be different, the silly philandering fool. She felt much better for having thus castigated him mentally.

She said suddenly, "Wouldn't you rather have had Abbie with you? You could go back for her, no matter what Jack said."

"No — impossible. Abbie is *persona non grata* with Beatrice at the moment. I don't want to risk them meeting. Though I sincerely hope Beatrice isn't around."

"Why is Abbie out of favour? Or can't you tell me?"

Dane started to chuckle. "Well, as a rule Beatrice is impervious to hints that she's speaking out of turn. But not this time. Josh was there. When you and Phyl were at the upholsterer's the other day, Beatrice drove over on some pretext or other. It's always a strain trying to be cordial to her. Talk turned to my books — we were trying to get her off the subject of Merle — and because I was dying to get back to my study, I said, 'Well, I must tear myself away. I'm drafting out a business letter to my publishers, concerning a contract. I must be sure I've got my facts and figures right.' And Beatrice said, 'Yes, I suppose now you're

157

in the TV field you have to watch your interest very closely, especially now you are spending so much on Inglethorpe House' and I'm blessed if she didn't ask, 'How much advance do you get on each book? Much more than at first, I imagine.'

"I was just working out the most tactful way of telling her that was entirely confidential, when Abbie, refilling Joshua's cup said, in one of her abstracted moments: 'That's it, Joshua. Remember that clue last night, two words, one starting with "c" and one starting with "i". The clue was contumely. It'll be "cool impudence".' It was so evidently what she was thinking, that it got through even Beatrice's thick skin. She put her cup down with a clatter and said huffily: 'Thank you very much for the insult — I thought that by now I might have been regarded as family and entitled to know!' and she walked out, got in her car and drove off in a spurt of dust.

"When I remarked, 'Abbie, I'd have thought of something myself, much more tactful', she said quite unrepentantly, 'but not half as effective', and even Joshua laughed: 'I agree, Abbie, Beatrice deserved her comeuppance. No one ought to ask a question like that.' "

Chloe said warmly, "I should think not."

"By the way, Merle had an appointment this morning with the parents of a girl in her class for disabled children but she was receiving them in the stables, in case Beatrice butted in. So we'll call there first."

Merle was just coming out as they drew up in front of the stables. Dane hugged her and dropped a kiss on one cheek. She said, "There's one thing, Beatrice is out, but Dad said we could have his study."

They came to the ranchsliders that were standing open as they approached the living-room. Beatrice *wasn't* out, she was on the phone, sounding very positive, as always.

They paused in the doorway, reluctant to interrupt and were prepared to retreat along the verandah to Jack's study when what she was saying registered with the three of them, though it didn't mean as much to Chloe as to the other two.

"No, Roddy, I strongly advise you not to contact Merle at present. This romance is at a very delicate stage. I did warn you of that when you rang last time. There's no chance for you now — how could you possibly compete with anyone earning as much as Dane is now? And, besides, they are so deeply in love it's a joy to behold. Do just accept this. If you really love her, you'll want to do what's best for her. She'll be just over the hill from her father and me, not traipsing all over the world in most unattractive and dangerous places seeking out rare species. Perhaps she should have told you instead of letting you cherish false hopes. But Roddy — don't —"

She got no further. An indescribable sound of fury — or disgust — had burst from Dane, and Chloe was aware that Merle had moved. But before either of them could do anything, the door at the other side of the room, nearer the phone, burst open and Jack Nathan, that man with the heart of butter, burst in. He seized the phone from Beatrice, said into it, "Roddy, for God's sake, hang on — none of this is true," then he bellowed: "You abominable woman — so this is why Merle thought Roddy had cooled off, that he must've met someone else! And she's fretting her heart out. Now, woman, march upstairs and pack your bags; you've been nothing but a she-devil all the years you've been here! Take every single thing you've got here — don't waste a moment — I want you out of here quicker than the speed of light. No, don't attempt explanations or excuses — get going before I do you physical harm."

He lunged towards her and Beatrice retreated towards the open door Jack had entered by. His voice followed her. "And don't imagine for a moment I'll relent. You can join your sister in that unit you both bought and if you tell her anything but the unvarnished truth, she'll hear it from me. Heaven help her having to put up with you." He paused a moment, took a stride towards the phone but became aware of the trio on the verandah.

Merle moved like lightning and her voice as she said, "Roddy, Roddy. So you care after all. Let me explain," was ringing with joy.

A deep voice answered her, "You don't have to, darling, I heard every word. I'm still reeling from the shock. Good for Jack. I'm coming home. We got held up in South America, in the jungle. Oh, my heart hasn't been in it the last few months. I thought how could I compete against anyone in the next bay, who's now a bestseller! But I decided to give it one more try. Look, I'm supposed to give a lecture in Boston next week on our findings but I'll cancel it or postpone it — I'll book a flight immediately. What did you say?"

Merle repeated her words. "*I'll* book a flight to *you*. Just give me an address. You aren't going to spoil one moment of your triumph. Besides, I can't wait — oh, Roddy."

Her father looked triumphant. "That's my girl! I'm off upstairs to speed the packing up. I don't want her under my roof a moment longer." He added, "Dane, the keys to Beatrice's car are on that key rack in the kitchen. Get her car out and bring it to the door. There is nothing she can say to excuse this. I want my home to myself right this moment."

Dane left at the double. Chloe, happiness breaking over her in waves, went out into the garden. It had been a fair morning before, but now the sky was blue, the bay greener, the birds singing more sweetly . . . Incident after remembered incident flashed through her mind. How ambiguous speech and happenings could be. She wandered out in a different direction from where Dane was parking Beatrice's car. It was nothing to do with her. She'd have liked to fold her tent like the Arabs and silently steal away.

Beatrice, with a white face and a mottled red neck, was attempting speech but Jack waved her down. "Not a word — you are an utterly malicious woman and a liar to boot. If you've left anything I'll send it after you — don't make it an excuse to come back. Right now I want to speak to my future son-in-law. That call of his must be costing him a fortune." He thrust two bulging cases into the back door of the car, said, "Now go!" and it could be said she stood not upon the manner of her going.

Jack disappeared inside again and Dane and Chloe were left looking at each other. She said, rather shakily because her own emotions were so tumultuous, "I feel as if a whirlwind has visited us, or a tornado. How absolutely unexpected. And who is Roddy?"

He gazed at her. "D'you mean Merle has never mentioned him to you? No, I suppose she wouldn't if she thought he'd let her down. He's Roderick Ffoulkes, just becoming recognised as an up-and-coming naturalist. He's the son of Jeremy Ffoulkes at Harvest Moon Bay. Remember, I pointed their house out to you once — it used to be the lodge of the hospital. Well — before it was a county hospital. Old Obadiah Cherrington had even more grandiose ideas than Aubrey. I believe there was some rivalry. I've been feeling angry with Roderick. I thought he *had* cooled off and there's never been anyone else for Merle from school days on. I thought that achieving some standing as the leader of this expedition had gone to his head, or else, as Merle thought, that he'd met someone else. Merle was all up-tight about it and when she met up with us at Harewood Airport she said to me, thank goodness I was back — she needed a confidante."

Chloe remembered that overheard snatch of conversation when Merle had said she was all right now. She took a tight rein on the thoughts that raced through her mind in bewildering succession. She mustn't give too much away. It mightn't add up to any more than the susceptibility of an author to whom words came too easily and who was only too apt to turn passing attractions into something that seemed like avowals of more meaningful emotions.

They went in to find the situation less awkward than it might have been. Jack was having a wonderful time on the phone to Roderick who didn't seem to care what it cost.

Merle, stars in her eyes and a tremble in her voice, came towards them, holding out her hands, and somehow Chloe got caught up in the tremendous hug Dane gave her. They heard Jack say: "I'll be very careful to get things right — too much has already gone wrong. Yes, I agree — much better to meet in Boston. I could believe anything after this — what a pair of fools you were

164

— I can imagine her finishing up in South America and you in the States. Oh, it's a case of London after Boston is it? Well, good luck to you, and I guess I'll have to take an interest in birds and winged insects for the rest of my life. Do you want me to contact Jeremy and Elizabeth for you? Might mean you haven't squandered all your award money on this toll call. Oh — you can't resist telling them yourself? Well, I can understand it — and my girl is tugging at my elbow. Beats me how she can find anything more to say. What's that — yes I'm sure you *would* like a few minutes privately with her; normally proposals aren't conducted with an eavesdropping audience. I'll take them all off to my office."

He waved Chloe and Dane out of the room ahead of him and they collapsed into easy chairs, and somehow found themselves laughing. Finally Jack sighed. "I'd no idea rage could be so exhausting. What'll you have, a brandy or gin and tonic? Sorry there's no champagne."

They had a short session with Merle when at last she tore herself away from the phone, then Chloe and Dane found themselves on their own, in the car, heading back to tell Abbie and Joshua, Phyl and Ross.

"I feel as if years must've passed since we

165

set out to come here," Dane said, as they crested the boundary hill. "For once I've had enough drama to satisfy me. Next time someone denigrates books and says 'of course things in that novel are highly exaggerated, they don't happen in real life' I shall smirk, say they're well off beam, that truth is indeed stranger than fiction, and look maddeningly mysterious."

"You chump!" said Chloe lightheartedly. "That's the author syndrome again. You see everything in terms of the realm of fiction. What are you stopping for? Have you seen a sheep in trouble or what?"

"It's not a sheep that's in trouble — it's you. You don't — can't, or won't — see me as anything else but an author. It's a grave handicap. But I would like you to think me more sincere. Tell me honestly, has Beatrice put this idea into your head? After what has happened this morning I can believe anything of her. Seeing she was engineering this situation did she warn you that I was a philanderer?"

Chloe had to be frank. "Not really, but she did lead me to believe that you and Merle had always been destined for each other."

"And you fell for it — you muggins!"

She fired up. "Well that makes two of us

166

— me and this Roderick Ffoulkes. If she could take *him* in, why not *me*?"

He made one of his exasperated sounds and the brows came down heavily in a scowl. "Well, I've been thinking him a fool ever since this happened."

"Thanks muchly. I'll excuse you for that insult on the grounds that none of us ever knows what sort of reaction someone else is having. This is the sort of situation I've been pitchforked into. You knew Beatrice far better than either me or this Roderick, I presume. How was I to know she was looking on me as a possible threat to her plans? I suppose that *is* how she regarded me!"

She saw the lines of laughter indent themselves about his mouth. "In the light of what she hoped for, she was right in that at least. But you've been so suspicious of every compliment I've ever paid you. Why?"

Her candour rose to the surface. "Well, a girl would naturally be suspicious of a man who suddenly flashed across a hitherto uneventful life, dazzling her like a meteor travelling across the sky and seemingly singling her out for his attentions — an ordinary person like me."

His surprise at this statement looked as if it was for real. "An ordinary person? I knew from the first day we met that you were a lass of mettle." His look was whimsical. He took her face between his hands, his eyes searching hers. "Chloe, you must be entirely without vanity. You've got eyes as green as the sea, hair like a flame, an intriguing row of freckles across your nose to save you from sheer perfection — which can be boring — the sort of chin that betrays a hint of a quick temper and, in some ways, you're a complete mystery to me. And don't you dare say *that* sounds like the description of a character between the pages of a book." His tone deepened, changed, "Now, tell me how on earth you could think those things about me after the day you found that sea horse?"

She was bewildered for a moment. He continued, "You don't know what I mean, do you? So it meant much less to you than to me . . . when I said that a kiss like that was a commitment. It was and still is. But it's much too soon. I could kill Beatrice — she's the one who has precipitated this. I like to do things in my own time — and perhaps in this case in *your* time. We're not all geared the same, I know, and I have my reasons." He grinned, the mischievous glint back in his eyes. "But perhaps actions do speak louder than words." And his mouth came down on hers and stayed there.

She came out of the enchantment of that moment — that long, loving moment — to be aware of something. Ross's estate car coming over the crest towards them. She freed herself, said, "Dane, Ross is coming. He must want you."

He did. There had been a phone call of some urgency from London. A reference had to be clarified, its source made clear. He was to ring Miles as soon as possible. Ross looked at them sharply, all of a sudden. "Is there anything wrong?"

Dane laughed. "No — I'm inclined to think everything is going rather well in the harbour. Beatrice has got her comeuppance — Jack has fired her lock, stock and barrel. She's on her way to Christchurch at this very moment with an outsize flea in her ear! Plus all her possessions. You know how quiet and reserved we thought Merle had become, and we wondered if Roddy had let her down, met someone else? Well he hadn't. Beatrice had made mischief. He rang from South America to try to get to the bottom of it. Beatrice answered the phone, not knowing we were all within earshot and gave the show away. Oh, I wish you had been there, Ross, when Jack called her an abominable woman! When a peace-loving man like him does lose his temper he does

169

it properly. It's all signed and sealed. Merle is to meet Roddy in the States — Boston — where he's to give a lecture to some famous society on his recent findings, then come back here for the wedding! Can you beat that?"

In an hour's time he had sorted out the problem in London, and all at Hauroko Bay were in possession of the facts.

Abbie said cheerfully, "If only Merle had confided in me. I'd have had it sorted out long ago." Her husband and his nephew couldn't speak for guffawing.

Chloe put her arms around Abbie and hugged her. "Of course you would have, darling. Take no notice of them. Everything has come out happily anyway."

Abbie returned the hug. "I'm so glad you came to Hauroko Bay. These two men would do me less than justice if you weren't here. They will harp on about my outspokenness and forget the times it's proved a blessing. If I hadn't offended Beatrice the other day Dane would probably have insisted on my going with him to Headland Bay." She addressed the two men. "It was better that Chloe should be there. She knows the true situation that way."

No one took that up, or asked why. Chloe felt relieved. She didn't want anyone delving

170

too deeply. Abbie added, "And do you know what Joshua said the other day? It was after I offended Beatrice. He said, 'My dear, if only you would engage your brain before you burst into speech.' I told him he sounded pompous and if there's one thing I can't abide in a man of the cloth it's pomposity."

They all burst out laughing. Joshua looked suitably humble. "Even after all these years she can still cut me down to size. My darling, it's okay. It *was* pompous and I wouldn't have you any other way even if at times you make me tremble in my shoes."

Abbie flushed with pleasure and said, "But now all is well between Roddy and Merle, and there's no grounds for misunderstanding between —" She hesitated, looked uncertain about finishing that sentence, then engaged her brain and said rather feebly, "— between Jack and anything he likes to do in the future."

Chloe knew relief. She had leapt to the conclusion that Abbie had noticed what she had been thinking, and the new understanding between Dane and herself was too fragile a thing to be taken for granted or commented upon.

She said briskly, "Now we can all get on with our particular jobs; Abbie and Josh helping Monica in the time she can spare from those consultations with Phyl — Monica is thrilled with some of the ideas they have, having already studied the drawbacks and advantages of houses built so long ago — I can finish what I'm doing for Ross and Phyl for Christmas, and harry the upholsterers to get those big deep old sofas finished, and Dane must shut himself into his study or we'll never again thrill to a new book by our favourite author."

He looked at her, grumbling mildly. "Only that last phrase redeems that speech. Has anyone ever told you that you are bossy?"

They laughed and departed to do exactly what she had suggested.

There was certainly more than enough to do and a lot of details must be attended to ahead of the 'Grand Opening' apart from the curtaining, carpeting, the finishing touches to all the re-plastering and papering that was now finished. In some of the rooms that had been largely unused till now, all sorts of treasures had been discovered, and hadn't been recognised as such till Chloe identified them. These were mostly things that dated back long before the early colonisation days and had been brought out to provide a touch of culture in a raw new land, no matter how beautiful in natural surroundings it had been. She even unearthed from the girls' playhouse some quite valuable Dresden china figures. A case of familiarity breeding contempt, she supposed.

Dane was most generous in parting with items from his own house to add to the atmosphere of the venture but Chloe demurred when he suggested transporting a beautiful corner cupboard displaying fragile china behind its diamond-paned leaded doors.

"It's so right here, in this small drawing-room. Headland House mustn't be stripped of all its glory for the sake of adding just one more touch over there for tourists."

He laughed. "We bow to your love of perfection, madam. I've got to admire your sense of the fitness of things. So be it. And I admit that I'd miss that particular piece."

It didn't matter that the walls of Inglethorpe House were rather crowded with pictures, as that had been the custom of the time. Many of them were of the old country the pioneers had left behind. Some were portraits. The one Chloe liked best was of 'old' Aubrey Inglethorpe and Caroline, his bride.

She said to Dane one day, "How strange

that they left all this and went back to Hampshire."

"Perhaps she was homesick. Perhaps both were. They made a great job of things in those earlier years and provided a good living for the families in the cottages. Pity that depression of the late Victorian era came along, and I dare say the outbreak of scab among their sheep worsened matters. But how hard to relinquish a dream. I wonder if they ever felt perfectly happy back in England again. I hope there were compensations. That Hampshire county is very beautiful of course. We are rather apt to forget that the isolation that separated them from all they'd hitherto held dear was something to be reckoned with!"

She said, "You mean those oceans of sea between all that was known and familiar — the time it took to get here. The difficulties of months at sea, the cramped conditions of shipboard life. The fear of epidemics that broke out, the awful loss of children, consigned to the deep in many cases. It must all have accentuated their homesickness."

He nodded. "It's good to remember these things, especially these days when we can cross those same seas and land in little more than twenty-four hours; when we can pick up a phone, dial a few numbers and be in

174

instant contact with relatives and friends — just think of waiting four or five months for a letter to be answered, the answers sometimes telling of a dear one whose earthly span had ended. To say nothing of fax machines making life easier for a poor bedevilled author trying to redeem some error he shouldn't have made, despite getting involved in someone else's love affair or getting distracted by his own emotions." He looked sharply at her. She seemed to be unaware.

"But it's a wise thing to remember when analysing one's reactions to living in another hemisphere that the world has shrunk, that there need not be the heartburnings of a century and a half ago."

Chloe didn't know if his tone was purposeful or not. Was she reading into such moments all she longed for? Wishful thinking?

She said briskly, "And I must remember that time flies just as quickly these days as it did then. Never enough hours in a day for all one hopes to accomplish. And when I look out at that row of houses that seem to be waiting for restoration for usefulness, I resent time going so fast."

He didn't take that up. She wished he had. He said, as if her words had recalled him to an awareness of the duty he owed to his publisher, "And if Miles could see me, he'd remind me of deadlines. So it's me for the word processor and the fax machine." He departed for his study.

There were hitches of course, to do with the redecorating; fabrics they particularly wanted were temporarily out of stock, picture frames suitable to the era in short supply, more red tape than they welcomed, insurances taken out, regulations to be satisfied; but in the main they left Dane to his study hours and attended to these things themselves. "After all," said Abbie, "that's what brings home the bacon. We could never have ventured upon this but for his success, and the farming was hardly ever breaking even. So much has depended upon him. But I predict that everything will come right for him."

Chloe wondered if everything would come right for *her*. In her more honest moments with herself, she admitted she was in danger of slipping into a happy daydream where life could continue on like this, without any termination. But how? Dane was so absorbed in his writing now, there had been no return to the tender moments of recently.

Then came the morning when he appeared before her with determination written all over him. "Come on, Chloe. I've asked Phyl and Monica if they need you for an hour or two, and none of the work the men are on requires your attention. We both need a break, so we're going up Headland Hill, down the gully and up the other side. It's quite a peak and gives you a glorious view." He looked at the sketches spread out in front of her on the old table. "I'm sure none of that is urgent. More embellishments than structural, I guess. Abbie said she'd put us up some sandwiches if you'd agree."

She stood up, stretched, said, "I guess you're right. I was getting stale over this. Were you feeling the same? Inspiration not flowing?"

"Not that, entirely, but the need to really relax away from the keyboard." He shrugged. "We pride ourselves on the advances, but years ago, all writers had to cope with was writer's cramp. Now we have to guard against OOS. I expect you know about it — occupational overuse syndrome. There is more known about it these days, but when I get right into the mood of a story, especially if the pace hots up and the chase is on, I find myself getting rigid and, though it's hard to tear oneself away, discipline is needed to make oneself desist. Like now."

"Well, if you really need the exercise I'll come. Sounds tempting anyway. Sometimes I find the urge to explore these hills and gullies almost too much for me. Do I need walking boots?"

"No, it's not as rugged as some areas. Steep but not intersected with great outcroppings of rock, or broken by cliffs. Those slacks will be fine. You'll need dark glasses though. The sun's very bright, and hot too, so you'd better take that linen sunhat as well. I'll get my pack for our lunch."

It was a day when nature seemed determined to make it one to remember. They paused on the long crest of the headland and looked down on both bays. Dane reflected. "Hard to realise that by tonight — our time — Merle will be having a joyous reunion with Roddy and making plans for an early wedding. Things are turning out very nicely. You weren't around when the gardener's wife put something to me yesterday. Jack would like her to work for him part-time. She's got her own car, so getting there is no problem. They're so keen to get settled in and save the daily drive from town they've intimated it would be no hardship to move in to the third house as it is — or nearly. I said they'd have to give me time to get the water and the electricity reconnected. Seems they were trying to raise a mortgage to buy the house they were renting, and this would take that burden off their shoulders."

They peered down the hillside. The relieving instructor Merle had been fortunate enough to find was walking horses out of the stable yard; the house lay bathed in sunshine, and wore a peaceful air, yet was a colourful blend of rioting scarlet geraniums, dark blue lobelia, delphiniums flaunting brilliant blue spikes of bloom in the back of the herbaceous borders, stone walls festooned with clematis, rosemary, virginia creeper, still green, that would be a glory in the autumn. They could distinguish Jack riding round his sheep with his head shepherd, a man at peace with his world.

Chloe turned away from it, looked down at Hauroko Bay, found herself saying, "But this is even more beautiful. I don't know what makes it like that. Perhaps the curve of the harbour waters indenting more, the avenue of hawthorns, even now they've stopped flowering; the utter charm of Inglethorpe House with its gables, its wide windows, the trees that cluster close as if

179

they wanted to be near it, that brook chattering over the stones, and Headland House somehow the epitome of the earliest days here. More intimate, less pretentious. I wonder if Aubrey and Caroline's happiest days were spent there, if the simpler life suited them better before they got caught up in what was, in essence, social climbing — probably very natural, each estate wanting to outdo the other, wanting to reach a sort of country squire standing such as they had coveted back home. Then the harder times came, they lost heart and returned to the scenes of their childhood. But how glad I am that other branches of the family returned to restore it to its old charm, to make it a viable concern."

Dane caught her hand as she stood there exulting in it, the breeze off the water outlining the feminine grace of her, blowing back the few tendrils that always escaped from that shining, copper plait. He sighed in contentment. "Not only the other branches of the family, but someone who might once have been described as a stranger in our midst . . . *you,* who has brought back so much of its former glory. To even that row of houses that has been regarded by us as a blot on the landscape but now is being brought into usefulness, and not only that, but something rather endearing. Oh look, Chloe, there's Joshua in the garden that will eventually be theirs. He's digging. That's the patch he said recently ought to have rows of blackcurrant and gooseberry bushes, and raspberry canes. It could be an old-fashioned kitchen garden bordered with hedges, and each side of a brick herringbone patterned path, all kinds of herbs. I feel herbs are once again getting the attention they deserve."

They saw Abbie go through the old wicket gate, obviously bearing a picnic basket that she set down beside an old willow. He smiled. "Having got rid of us they're celebrating in the nicest way possible. Having lived so long in vicarages that were never their own, never feeling free to throw out a window here, add a porch there, or ranch-sliders, they're getting a big time out of this, bless them. I must do all I can to see they realise their dream before too long."

Chloe didn't meet his gaze. She said instead, "Which way now?"

"Over the creek on these stepping stones, and through that patch of bush. There's a track leads from it up the shoulder of the hill."

Half an hour later she was saying breathlessly, "I thought you said this wasn't a tough climb — and how on earth do we scale that massive out-thrust of rock up there?"

He laughed. "We don't. There's a track leads round it. Then you'll count it all worthwhile, I promise."

They scrambled on up. The tussock was slippery but spectacular, blown silver in the sun, contrasting strikingly with the sea below that was more blue than green today.

They finally reached the top. She was enchanted to find that from here you could see way down south — a seemingly boundless rim of ocean and a lavender horizon for a hundred miles and more.

She dropped to the ground, having gazed her fill and said in awe: "What a place to live!"

"Exactly," stated Dane.

Chapter Seven

Pangs of hunger attacked them and they did full justice to Abbie's beef sandwiches, her delicious slabs of cold pie, the coffee and gingerbread, with a pack of their first strawberries.

Above them a lark sang, hardly discernible as even a speck in the sky. They were leaning back against a cabbage tree that had survived the winds that beat up the harbour, drowsily content with sun and expended energy. Chloe ventured an observation. "I love New Zealand birds; of course the tui's song is, as you say, like a woodland harp, the bellbird and the *riroriro* we heard in the gully that you said sings more sweetly after rain, but oh how glad I am that there are so many English birds, known and familiar, and dear. Most of all the skylark. It sounds like the very essence of happiness itself."

Dane rolled over on one elbow and regarded her. "You've just reminded me of something that happened in London. I couldn't believe it. I was in Hyde Park, but there was the roar of traffic close by and the chatter of countless thousands that go to make up the population, when suddenly in a rare still moment, I heard it . . . a lark, high in the heavens, singing as if its throat would burst, and I recalled a fragment of poetry I'd read in one of Gran's scrapbooks when I had measles and had run out of reading matter. It seemed to me as if that moment long ago, and the one in Hyde Park met, and was meant to meet. As if that unknown poet and I had shared the same moment perhaps sixty years apart; as if time stood still. Want to hear it?"

She sat up a little. "*Do* I? I should think I do."

He said, "It was called just that 'A Skylark in London' and went:

'Into the city streets this stranger
    brings
His country song; above the traffic's
    flow
He climbs on cool and uncorrupted
    wings,
Oblivious of the restless world below,
And where his ancestors once sang, he
    sings
Of summer days a thousand years ago.'

It was by a Douglas Gibson. I've never come

across anything else of his. I don't know when he lived or where he lived except for that one day when he and I were caught up in a feeling of timelessness, and I felt I shared it with all those people who had heard a lark singing its heart out through the centuries. And here today, you and I shared it, all because you put your thoughts into words. Thank you, Chloe."

He leaned closer, looked into those sea-green eyes, kissed her, then said, "For once you've not spoiled the moment by saying it's probably grist to the mill." She had no answer for that, but he was continuing any-way. "I made up my mind that today I'd tell you the full story of the girl who couldn't take the change from the old world to the new. Just in case you ever have any doubts about it."

Doubts? What could he mean? Why her? Did he mean doubts that the story had been exaggerated? Or . . . did he mean he wanted her to know that homesickness was a force to be reckoned with? Then — did he think he might persuade her to *stay?* Or was she reading too much into it? She hadn't time to think that out because he began.

"It was away back in the Edwardian days when London was a gay place, one of parties and theatres, of elaborate dresses and ridiculous hats and those were the circles she moved in."

You knew he was a storyteller when he talked like this. "Not that her people came from London — they came from Northumberland, but she'd spent two years in the metropolis with an aunt who was addicted to the theatre, to balls, to musical concerts. She had had the occasional letter from Gregory Inglethorpe who'd been a playmate of her childhood years and was flattered when he sought her out. He was a very handsome man. I think he talked more of the gay colonial life of years before. She got swept off her feet, the aunt gave them a fabulous wedding and no alarm bells sounded for either her or Gregory.

"She had nothing of the hardships of the women who came out by sailing ship. Their passage was by steamer of course. It came up from the south, round Bluff and right into Lyttelton Harbour. She appreciated the beauty of it, we believe, but the isolation then of Hauroko Bay appalled her. If only Gregory had lived in Christchurch which from very early days had known a culture very different from the remoteness of the bay — in fact here they relied a great deal on water transport from Lyttelton, and there were no understanding neighbours near. For her the songs on the wind sang only sad songs. The eerie whistling got on her nerves. Someone once said that to hear her playing her violin was heart-rending — all the laments, the strongly national tunes of the old country.

"Gregory loved the life here so much he didn't seem to understand it. He was a tireless worker and needed to be. He saw other women fitting in, and felt that in time she would get over the extreme nostalgia. He didn't realise she had a real sickness of the heart. He couldn't believe it when she announced, after evidently a long time of soul-searching, that she was going home. He felt that as so often happens she would find people and places so changed, even that her niche in people's affections had gone, but that didn't work for him. Her aunt had died, she returned to her people in Northumberland and it seemed a deadlock.

"Gregory missed her heartbreakingly, but he remained adamant that she must fit into his life. That was the way of things then. But out of the blue, after a time when even no letters passed between them, some Christchurch friends of his had a trip to England. They met her in a Tyneside street, very obviously pregnant. They did their best for her and for Gregory. She told them she thought had she known about the child she had so longed for she would never have left him. It would, she thought, have helped banish her loneliness; but she would never want Gregory to think that she came back to him because of the baby. Of course, these people came back, went to see him, and Gregory didn't hesitate. He got someone in to manage the farm and took a passage for England and just turned up at her parents' residence. He offered to come back to England — he opened up in a way he never had before. He was delighted about the child. Her parents were so happy about it. Marriage break-ups were rare then. But before a week had passed Gregory was dead. This unsuspected heart defect. I believe she was beside herself with remorse and regret, thinking that the stress she had caused him had brought this about.

"Now Gregory, before he took passage, had made a strange will here. Whether he knew or suspected he had something wrong with him we'll never know, but this will left his property to his wife and child-to-be, either son or daughter. But when the executors in New Zealand tried to trace them, it proved impossible — perhaps because the First World War broke out then. For whatever reason, that was how our branch of the family finally took it over, but the proviso remained. My paternal grandfather tried from time to time, but searches were always thwarted in some way. You'd have thought a name like Inglethorpe could have been found, but no. Legal provision was made though, that even after all this time, some sort of settlement could be made if a descendant of that child was traced. It could have been overturned, but our side, I'm proud to say, always felt it would be only fair to allow for the unlikely — perhaps some descendant, feeling they'd been cheated out of a birthright, to put it dramatically. However, it hardly seems likely now. I did some looking-up in old records when I was over there, and when I got further involved in signing sessions and then contracts re television rights, Josh and Abbie did a bit of research. All to no avail. The trail was too old and it seemed a lot of records were lost up north during the bombing in the Second World War."

Chloe didn't speak right away. She had drawn her knees up and clasped her hands around them, looking out across the harbour waters. Then: "It's a sad story, Dane, but you've done all you could. Plenty wouldn't have bothered. Why did you feel I must hear this?"

"I don't know. I felt impelled to tell you. I think anyone who exchanges one world for another should know homesickness can play the very devil with newer loyalties."

There was a long silence. Chloe felt she didn't know where to go from here, how to react. She decided to be noncommittal, and without giving away how moved she was, or asking any questions, she said as lightly as she could, "Well, it's all a long time ago, Dane, and evidently your grandfather did all he could. I admire all of you for not dropping the search, and surely to goodness there's little likelihood of anything cropping up now." She had to add something else, something that if Dane had the purpose in telling her this that she hoped he might, could reassure him, "And it's not *everyone* who can't take on a new life. It's a different age, a different world, one that has shrunk in terms of time if not distance. I did hear Josh saying something of this the day we went to Portchester Castle but didn't dream it was so sad a story. I thought it was just a matter of looking up something for a family tree. I suppose she went back to London, even if her aunt was gone, or might have left Northumberland for any other place — perhaps wanting to go somewhere where her story wasn't known if she felt so badly that the stress Gregory had suffered had short-ened his life."

Chloe stood up, unwilling for him to go into his reasons for telling her. There was far too hectic a time ahead, the last of the restoration undertakings to be gone into, Phyl and Ross's preparations for Christmas and the week following that for the grand opening of a venture she hoped for all their sakes, was successful.

"I did promise Phyl I'd do a soufflé for the dinner we're having over there tonight and sort out something with the foreman about next week's work, so we should make our way down now, don't you think? I'm sure this has kept you away from the com-puter long enough to save you being threat-ened with overexposure."

There was no more talking. The scramble down was very slippery, the tussocks were dry and they had to negotiate the stepping stones over the creek more carefully from this side because the water swirled against the bank making the first steps more haz-ardous. They both slipped in, with great splashing, but finally, now quite tired, they reached Headland House and welcome showers. Although the foreman had gone and Chloe had to hustle in the kitchen of the big house to time her soufflé, Joshua and Abbie were already there looking happy and relaxed after their picnic and gardening in their home-to-be.

There were other days, of course, that were sheer hard grind, days when nothing went right with their schemes, but that was only to be expected with something so ambitious. Phyl was wonderful. There must have been times when the very magnitude of the task daunted her, but as long as she didn't feel the children were neglected she seemed able to face anything. Chloe remarked on it wondering how she could stand up to it, even retain her sparkle when she talked about it. Phyl's eyes were darker than Dane's tawny ones, but lit up just as his did when he wanted to share something with them about his new book.

When Chloe commented on her undiminishing zest, Phyl laughed. "But it's so wonderful to see a dream coming true. With the farming economy so different from what it used to be, I dreaded the day when Ross might have to leave here to take on a farm manager's job — which would have broken his heart . . . and mine. I've never lived anywhere else. Life here is woven into the very tapestry of my being, and I so want it for my children. It's ideal for them — the horse paddocks for Sarah, the sea and shore for Pip. I've this feeling that some day she'll be known for her expertise in marine life just as Roderick Ffoulkes is known for his, and they'll visit Merle's father so often he'll be right on the spot for her, and Merle for Sarah. Besides, as Mother always used to say, there'll be kingfisher days amidst all the humdrum ones when we have to plug away at duty; halcyon days."

Chloe said, "Oh, how I wish I'd known your mother. She must've been like Dane, able to handle words."

"Yes, she was Gran's daughter most dramatically in that. I'm so glad she saw the first dawning of success coming Dane's way. She would have loved you, Chloe."

Chloe found she was colouring up and said hastily, "What exactly did she mean by halcyon days? So few people use that word."

"Oh, she loved the little-known meaning of it. Halcyon is an old name for the kingfisher which was once believed to make a floating nest upon the sea which remained calm when hatching, so halcyon days were those that were peaceful, happy, serene. When she married Dad and left the plains so far inland she loved the maritime flavour of the bay, and the kingfishers that nested in the clay of Headland Cliff. It's not all rock, you know. Get Pip to show you. Mother said that on days when skies were at their bluest and even tinged the green harbour waters, that they were kingfisher days."

Chloe's eyes were sparkling now. "I know what I'll do — there's that book on birds in the little sitting-room. I wonder if Dane would let me cut a picture of one out and frame it to join the others in those panels between the windows. The colours would be perfect. Dane was the one who had the idea of using that long-ago photo of your father as a boy, driving the team of draughthorses *his* father had won awards for."

"That's a lovely thought. Sometimes I can't believe both parents are not still here to share in the delight of this. Especially when we've still got Gran and Grandad. They're coming over for Christmas dinner as usual. Said they'd understand if they had to forgo it this year with the grand opening so near but I can't let that custom be dropped."

Chloe hugged her. "I do love you, Phyl, and admire you for preserving the things that matter in the midst of all the necessary commercialism that is inescapable from a venture like this. Though it's not all a way of making a living. The workmen are so fired with enthusiasm they're doing a great job of advertising by word of mouth. And having Barry and Monica on the spot now has greatly eased the burden. They, like the gardener and his wife, have taken a load off Dane's shoulders and it did worry me to see him spending so much time out of his study."

Phyl's look was shrewd. "They're not the only ones to have eased the burden. Dane said the other day you're by way of a gift to a poor harassed author, that in the times you're not over here, you look up quotations and references for him — to say nothing of coming out with things from your own experiences that he's found very inspiring."

Chloe knew a glow, then a chill as she thought of her return to England, when life as lived at the bay would be only a memory. There had been no more tender interludes . . . but then both had been so busy, she with her drawings and plans in that bare little room under the eaves, he with the so necessary absorption in the current book, to say nothing of the business affairs she hadn't realised intruded so much into his working hours. Joshua and Abbie seemed to spend much more time across at the village these days. She wondered about that, but Joshua said, with that endearing twinkle in his eyes that were so like Lucy, his mother's, "Of course the soil over there is much more fertile and takes a lot less watering. You should see my lettuces, and the tomatoes and strawberries are far ahead of the Headland House ones. My potatoes are going to be just as I like them for Christmas, not too large, not too small. Well, it will seem very strange to you, Chloe, that there will be no berries on the holly — but the Australian bottlebrush will provide us with scarlet for the decorations, and fir trees are the same the world over. We often have turkey, same as in England, but this year Phyl wants to practise producing colonial goose ready for the menu for New Year's Day and the grand opening. Has she told you of it? Legs of lamb boned and stuffed — the boning is a horrid job and it's falling to me. I'm going to do ever so many for the new deep freeze. There'll be plenty of chickens too, ducklings and hams of course."

Chloe also found out that for the family Christmas dinner, it was traditional to have plum puddings, but fruit salad and trifles were served for the children who always wanted a swim early afternoon and wouldn't be allowed to if they indulged in the puddings. She was delighted to know that Joshua always conducted a nine o'clock service in the little village chapel that was called St Chad's. It was quite a tradition for the people of the over-harbour bays to attend, and holidaymakers would swell the numbers. Other services would be held at Holy Trinity in Lyttelton, a beautiful mellow edifice older even than Christchurch Cathedral, which was natural, as Lyttelton had been the port of entry for so long.

Dane had to leave the gathering of the evergreens — from that gully they had clambered through the day of their picnic — to Ross, his man and the gardener. Packets of mail marked urgent had arrived that week and he'd had to shut himself into his study from morning till night, and consequently Chloe felt rather flat. Their tree was a beautiful sight, grown on the estate, and the children were wildly excited, eyeing the heap of parcels at the foot with great speculation and from time to time appearing with extra parcels to be deposited there too.

Now they were in bed, and dusk and a sense of peace had enfolded the darkening bay with purple wings. It was unbearably hot and they were all tired. Dane had been in his study all day, Joshua was in his own little workroom going over his readings, and

Abbie was making a pavlova to take across the next day.

Suddenly Dane appeared, freshly showered and looking not at all like a man who had spent long, stuffy hours at his desk. "All is finished," he declared, "now I can enjoy Christmas. I'll drive round to Lyttelton the day after Boxing Day with that pile of revised manuscript."

"Couldn't you just send it over by one of the launches?" asked Chloe.

He looked horrified. "No, even though I've a good photocopy, I take no risks with it finishing up at the bottom of the harbour. It represents too much sweat and toil, and after I see it safely dispatched the rest of the week belongs to Phyl. I started this project and I must see it through. But this is a strange Christmas Eve for you. It's not far off midnight's witching hour. Come on outside."

She went willingly. They saw the lights at Inglethorpe House go out and presently the one in Abbie and Joshua's room. Those at Lyttelton sparkled across the water, and the strains of 'Silent night, holy night' were borne to them on the wings of that caressing wind that so often owed nothing to human voices, but whispered of the past and had a magic all its own.

The incomparable sound of gentle waves lap-lapping at the shore added its own perfection to the night and the air was cool against their foreheads. Now and then a sleepy bird twittered and the bowl of the summer sky, like navy-blue velvet, was a-glitter with stars. One star was so prominent they could imagine it was the Star of Bethlehem. As they passed beside the gate that bordered the rose garden, the perfume of their blooms and the Christmas lilies drifted up to them, and far across the water the church bells rang out as worshippers poured out of Holy Trinity.

Dane took her hand for the short walk to the front door, standing hospitably open to the cooler air. They mounted the stairs. They paused at the door to her room. He took her by the shoulders, turned her round so the light from the skylight fell across her face. "Thank you for helping our dream come true. Merry Christmas and good-night." His kiss was light. It seemed the right sort of kiss for the first hour of Christmas Day. Chloe wondered where she would be next Christmas . . . it gave her a strange sensation of loneliness. She knew why. It wasn't the beauty of this place, the spell it had cast over her. It was Dane himself. Any future she might envisage for herself was bleak indeed if he wouldn't be part of it. She dismissed the thought, impatient with herself. This was Christmas Day and the joy of seeing the girls open their presents wasn't far ahead, and being part of the local service at St Chad's in the lovely little church whose interior, because they looked upon it as the house of God, was the one example of meticulous care and maintenance. Abbie would be playing the organ and Chloe would have Dane beside her, his baritone matching her contralto in the same hymns her people in Surrey would be singing, albeit later, because it was still Christmas Eve afternoon with them.

She had got Sarah a model of a young foal, on a stand, for her bedroom, and in her script she used for wall texts had printed 'Heloise' across the base, but Pip's present her mother had mailed her from Chloe's own bedroom above the antique shop, something she'd had from her Tyneside childhood, a little brass sea horse, a replica of the one on the Newcastle upon Tyne coat of arms. The children were rapt over these unusual gifts.

Dane's to her was unusual too, at least to her. It was a greenstone *tiki*, the beautiful New Zealand jade, and had come from the West Coast. It was translucent, so that the light shone through it. Dane fastened it about her neck and it changed with every movement she made. The carving was intricate and she suspected it was very old. A reward for restoring Inglethorpe House perhaps, or — ? What did she hope? There was a line in one of Dane's books she had liked when she read it first, two years or so ago. The hero had said, 'The only meaningful present from a man to his love is, of course, jewellery. Something to set its seal upon her finger, or to lie against her throat like a caress.' But of course that had been fiction and the incident he'd dreamed up to suit the story had been charged with emotion for the purposes of the story. Her frock was the same green as the *tiki*. Not by happy coincidence but because he had said to her the day before, "Do wear that green frock for Christmas dinner that you wore when I took you to Harvest Moon Bay to meet Jeremy Ffoulkes, Rod's father, and Elizabeth, his stepmother."

Chloe had loved them both. Elizabeth was a great favourite of Dane's. Naturally, because she was another author, but more because he knew that years before, she had made such a pal of a lonely little boy, and encouraged him so much in his forays into remote bushland, in search of rare birds; he was now known across the world as an expert. Jeremy was the editor of the *Argus* and had given the restoration of Inglethorpe House and its plans for the future the sort of publicity that was unbelievable. He knew every detail of the Church of England colony and he'd caught fire from his appreciation of the way Chloe had identified herself and her art with the early days. He was to be the guest speaker at the opening but had decreed the people must eat first, then hear his speech which, he told them, was not to be of any length.

Dane had said, "How lucky can we get, and isn't it well timed? Merle and Roddy's engagement is to be announced in the paper the day before. His sketches of native birds that he lent us will be of particular interest because of it."

The great day came and was a huge success. Not just a magnificent meal, served at one-thirty so guests could wander round the bay and gardens in daylight, but most seemed thrilled with the links with other years . . . the First Four Ships; the photos of the terrific effort of the young, far from healthy colony, to raise a worthy cathedral in the heart of the city; every aspect of the harbour in sketches and photographs; some touching mementoes of Captain Scott and his gallant comrades; some prints of Peter Scott's bird studies, the son of the famous man, who had been deprived of his father so early in his life; and Chloe had sketched Ripa Island and a likeness of the admirable Count von Luckner. She had done it imaginably and because she so liked the story of his not sinking any ships till every crew member and the ship's cat were saved, she'd executed a sketch of a very happy cat, with under it a caption: 'Who then is my enemy?'

Success was assured, the summer tourist season was ahead of them, and Phyl had even been approached as to the likelihood of weddings and balls being held there. Chloe was thrilled for Dane's sake; he had sunk so much of his hard-earned money into it.

Once the place was well launched he spent many early morning hours working in his study from five A.M. When she remarked on it he grinned and said: "I had the best possible training for that, rising early for mustering, shearing, drafting, tailing and lambing."

The children went back to school in early February, leaving on the bay's school bus at eight every morning. Merle wrote from London that she and Roddy would like their wedding to take place at St Chad's, Joshua officiating of course, and the reception at Inglethorpe House, though it wouldn't be till after Easter.

Dane asked Chloe to stay on till after then. "I'd appreciate you overseeing the interior decorating of Josh and Abbie's place, Barry and Monica's and Gordon and Sylvia's. It was so good of both those last two pairs to move in before the houses were really fit to live in — and I'm sure you'd like to see that village street at least partially restored."

Partially? Then he didn't expect her to see it complete! Chloe felt lower than low.

He shut himself away rather more than was sensible, driving himself too hard, she felt. But then authorship meant deadlines and understanding from his family. But when he emerged, stretching himself and saying, "Let's climb the Giant's Face — are you game?" she always went willingly. It wasn't all work and climbing though. Occasionally he took her to the lovely Town Hall, with its fountains playing on the waters of the Avon, with famous singers on stage, or some opera company. She found he, too, loved plays best, the spoken word. Also that Shakespearean ones were his favourites above all.

She helped Abbie with the cooking. "As long as you don't expect me to turn out the sort of concoctions Phyl does. I was brought up in the good old north of England way. Steak and kidney puddings, hotpots, plain roasts."

Abbie gave her a hug. "Best of all I love the way you make a huge Yorkshire pudding, to have with the roast beef, not those fiddly little ones, and you make enough to have it for a dessert afterwards, with golden syrup — the real Northumberland way. Oh, I may have lived the other side of the border but my childhood holidays were spent at Hexham. And Dane loves your dumplings in your stews. Doughboys as you call them."

Dane announced to her one evening, when they were fishing off the rocks at Headland Point, that it was necessary for him to take a short trip to England on business. She held her breath. Would this mean he might say, "How about finishing up here? Then you'd have company on the trip back." But he didn't.

She ventured, "Knotty problems, Dane? Ones that can't be ironed out with phones and faxes?"

"Not really. There are things I would rather see to personally, and that's what I'm telling the others, because I don't want Phyl and Ross thinking this might be a threat. You remember I'd pursued an unfruitful line regarding that will of Gregory Inglethorpe's and his possible descendants? Well the agency I employed — one that does a lot of research — has suddenly found something while investigating things for another client. I feel I must see to it, though by now I'd rather it wasn't a complication. I wish I'd not triggered this off. I'll go to see your people, of course. In fact I wondered, if your parents are so well settled in now, if your grandmother might like to pay a visit here? She was so interested in this place."

Chloe was radiant. "What a wonderful idea. But not yet, Dane. I'd like to see that village more complete — she was so taken with it, intrigued, even."

He nodded. "But I'll put it to her." The radiance dimmed as she anticipated the bay without Dane for weeks on end. Three days later he told them he had the chance of an earlier flight than anticipated. "Then I'll be back all the sooner Chloe, and hopefully I'll have a mind at rest."

The day before he left he came into what they all called 'Chloe's cubbyhole'. She was busy at her table. He looked around.

"I've spoken to Barry about this room. He agreed with me that it's out of place for the brain behind the transformation of Inglethorpe House to work in these surroundings, so while I'm away, I've asked him to do it up if you can stand the noise and disruption."

"It's hardly worth it, Dane, for the few weeks left. And with the whole panorama of Lyttelton Harbour through that window, who wants it adorned?"

He didn't reply directly to that. She'd hoped he would. He merely said in a very ordinary tone, "Oh, Roderick Ffoulkes rang me from London yesterday and put a proposition to me. Merle would like to continue the riding school and doesn't want to be too far away from New Zealand. Rod's main work will always be in this country. It seems Jack's been most enthusiastic about what you're doing with the village street. Talks a lot to them by phone and they are sold on the idea of living in one of the houses. So, you'll be here for some time yet."

He was very matter-of-fact about it. "I've always felt badly about you working in such dingy surroundings. I thought that paper we used for the Captain Scott room, almost white with the faintest hint of ice-blue would be just right for here. But you're the expert

207

— how does it appeal to you?"

Her eyes lit up. "Oh, I can just see it. You must have a hidden talent yourself in these matters!"

He continued on. "And you know our old playroom downstairs. It has that old-fashioned Wilton carpet on the floor, grey with a design of blues and mauves. Perhaps it would satisfy that frugal slant of yours, to use that instead of plain wall-to-wall. I'm attached to it. Dad and I made fleets of fretwood cars and the border made wonderful tracks to run them on. But perhaps you'd have other ideas?"

"No — sounds just right to me. It will be lovely, though it's an extravagant idea, apart from the carpet. I'm quite happy with just a bare workroom and I don't worry if I splash paint about when I'm working at my easel. I'd have to be more careful if you bring that carpet up."

"You can spread hessian under the easel and train yourself to be more tidy, my girl."

She liked the sound of that. A careless term meaning nothing, of course, but how sweet if it had had a deeper meaning. In any case, though he knew it not, she was his, body, soul and spirit.

He walked about suggesting various things, then came back to look over her shoulder. She was adding a name to a painting of a tui she'd done previously. It was sitting on a flax bush in the garden, and she'd caught the gleam of the sun on the white feathers at its throat and its iridescent plumage.

He said, "I can see Roddy asking you to illustrate one of his bird books. You have the touch." She looked up at him to ask if he really meant that, but was halted by noticing that devil-may-care look in his eye. He stared at her accusingly. "You've tied your beautiful hair back with a bootlace — it's almost a sacrilege."

She said, "Oh, don't be so stupid. I can't bear it falling over my face as I work and my plait wouldn't go right this morning. I wish it was straighter and smooth. Bits were sticking out all over."

One tug and the bootlace was gone. Another touch, a ruffling one, and her hair was all about her.

"You have such exuberant hair — as if it had a life and a will of its own."

She burst out laughing. "Don't you know why? I read once that red hair is more thick and springy because it's some percentage or other more coarse than other hair."

Dane shook his head. "I don't believe that. Yours shines from that widow's peak right down to the way it curls up at the ends."

She shrugged. "Miles will find your descriptions of your female characters more convincing now. Off with you. I want to finish this."

"I can do more than describe them. Other things in that area come more easily too. This, for instance," and the next moment he was kissing her, pulling her to her feet and holding her close. Then he released her a little. His breath was warm on her cheeks.

"That will do for our goodbye kiss when Ross takes me to the airport. The whole darned family will be there and I'll have to content myself with a chaste peck."

"Or we could shake hands," she suggested demurely. She had to lighten the situation because she didn't want him to guess how weak her knees seemed, or feel the thudding of her heart.

He brought both hands up under her coppery hair and fluffed it out. "Much more artistic," he commented, and turned to the door. He paused there, his hand on the knob, then said quite deliberately, and audaciously. "Do you know how your hair would look best of all?"

"No, I don't and I don't regard you in

any way as a connoisseur of women's hair-styles."

"Oh, not of styles. Don't you want to know how I best like to picture your hair?"

"No, I don't. You are in a mad mood."

"But I'll tell you just the same. I'd like to see it loose, spread out on a white pillow, preferably mine."

He laughed at the look on her face and said, "I'm not propositioning you. It's just my artistic talent rising to the top," and he was gone.

He had roused longings in her she'd rather be without and she didn't know how she could endure the next few weeks without him.

Chapter Eight

The girls took it for granted that with Dane away Chloe had more time to spend with them after school and Phyl stopped feeling guilty when she wasn't working, then saying, quite truthfully, that it eased her own burden.

One day, Chloe, fossicking for shells in a pool at high tide spotted a sea horse for Pip to hold for a few delighted moments before lovingly depositing it where there was no chance of being stranded. Pip said, dark eyes aglow, "Chloe, it makes me feel I can now believe in that strange book in the old library about the ancient sea monsters, but this is one I think must've been changed by the fairies into something smaller — what's the word I want?"

Chloe thought. "I think you mean miniature, and perhaps the gods knew we'd love it more as small as this, and not be afraid. You ought to write an essay on it, Pip. Look it up in the encyclopaedia, that way it's based on fact. I do know it's a most extraordinary creature because the male is the one that gives birth — sort of coughs it up out of a little pouch. If you like to really study it, then, keeping the facts right, weave a little story about it to interest children; I would illustrate it for you. But first of all I'll do you a picture of one to hang on your wall." Pip gave her a rapturous hug that smelt strongly of sea water, rotting seaweed, and fish scales.

They had caught some quite large herrings and intended to ask Abbie to cook them for a special breakfast at Headland House. They had no inhibitions about asking themselves over. "And Uncle Josh will gut them for us. And Abbie cooks herrings beautifully. Mum says they're too fiddly. But wait till I tell them about the sea horse. That it wriggled in my hand!"

Chloe looked at the little, earnest face. "I know a poem from my great-granny's scrapbook, about sea horses. I know it by heart. Like to hear it?"

She didn't say it all, as she had to Dane, that day on the beach. It suddenly occurred to her Pip would demand to know of the first words, why guilt, and Chloe didn't know herself. She had often wondered about it. Perhaps some misdemeanour in Greeny's young days, something that wouldn't matter now, but would have then. She'd never asked Leonora about it because Leonora, she believed, had adored Greeny and wouldn't like to besmirch her memory in any way.

Pip said, "Go on, Chloe, you've gone into a daydream."

Chloe smiled. "Well, I realised I remember the last half best. Someone must have asked Greeny what magic was. So she wrote this poem to tell them. Or perhaps she wrote it just to satisfy herself. Here goes — this is the last half:

'So what is magic? Sun and moon and
    wind,
The glimpse of hills when morning mists
    have thinned . . .
The tranquil waters where the tall ships
    ride,
The treasures that were mine with every
    tide,
Sea horses, starfish, oyster shells and
    more,
Washed to my feet upon that far-flung
    shore . . .
Magic? Go find it, lest it pass you by
The sun, the sea, the moon, the starlit
    sky.' "

Pip stood there, quite silent, the skirt of

her gingham dress soaked to her thighs. She put a hand to her immature chest, said wonderingly, "I don't know why but it makes me feel — sort of funny here. It's so beautiful it almost hurts." She looked around. "It's as if it was written about here, about our bay. I love it. Was she a great traveller? I suppose it could be anywhere in the world."

"It could be," said Chloe, "but we'll never know. She died so long ago. I just remember her. I think she lived by the sea in the north of England. My grandmother used to say no one cooked a herring like her. She said she used to stuff them with bread, onion and sage and tie thread around them. Let's tell Abbie — though she'll probably say we'd better do them ourselves. If so, we jolly well will. Come on. We'll prepare them tonight and have them tomorrow. Nice to look forward to, plus the fact Barry was to start getting my cubbyhole ready today so he could start papering tomorrow. We'd better get back."

Barry had done more than he'd anticipated. The walls had been stripped earlier, but he'd already got one wall papered. The windows looked much bigger now they were framed in the white paper with the tinge of ice-blue. He was delighted with Chloe's reaction. Pip had gone home to do her homework.

"I've never felt so much satisfaction in my life before, as now, here at the bay," Barry uttered. "I'm even enjoying my spare time as never before, doing up our place. If it hadn't been for you, we'd never have thought of it, but you saw it all so clearly in your mind's eye, we began to visualise it too. I can't think of a better life. That early morning swim tones you up for the day. I expect there's a lot you miss about England but I guess having a sea water swimming pool right at your front door makes up for a lot. Aren't you glad your favourite author came to the UK and kidnapped you?"

She hoped she'd never have to tell him it was, after all, just a job!

He said, "I can't believe how lucky we are about these window frames. To discover they are solid kauri, as good as the day they were put in. They built to last in those days. Wonderful timber, so slow-growing. If only we had more forests of it left! The old mariners prized it for their masts. I wonder if the trees these came from in the North Island were felled before its great value was discovered or how much they cost. Then they'd have to be shipped down here. Made me feel like Captain Cook discovering New

Zealand when I realised these were of kauri."

"Careful, Barry, you'll infect me with your enthusiasm, and before you know it, I'll be planning a Captain Cook room. Bank's Peninsula has all the ties with him, named for his great naturalist, Joseph Banks."

"You could make that the theme for this room. It doesn't all have to be over at Inglethorpe House, this was nearer his time, anyway."

"It's not over to me, Barry. It's not *my* house."

He gave her a long, considering look, then, "I reckon the boss would let you do anything you liked with this."

She achieved a shrug. "I wonder what this room was used for in the very early days? Do you think it was just an odd structural corner that was merely the easiest way to get up to the tower?"

"May have been. I believe that was erected quite some time after the house was built, due to a whim of some family connection, a retired admiral who came out here to visit the nephew of Aubrey's who took it over when Aubrey went back to England. The old fellow wanted to be able to use his spy glass from it, to see all the shipping that entered the harbour. They had the money till scab attacked their sheep, and the rabbit menace worsened. Phyl told me this."

"Oh Barry, that's marvellous. I can just imagine the admiral pacing up there, imagining he was on his own quarterdeck."

He was back the next morning; Chloe found he didn't hinder her work at all. It was one of those days when the light on the water was forever changing, as the sun emerged now and then from the cotton-wool clouds of the sky.

He had stopped to cut more paper as an extra bright gleam struck across the room to the wooden staircase. He made an exclamation and went across to it where the side was boarded up. He ran his hand downward and said, quite excitedly. "I thought so! There *is* a cupboard here — nearly all stairs have a cupboard underneath them. This one's been plastered over and that old-fashioned dark green paper is so thick we've not noticed it before. I'll have a go at it tomorrow. This afternoon I'm needed elsewhere." He grinned. "At best we might find some priceless antique or a valuable picture. At worst mouldering relics of unwanted furniture. Perhaps those old deck chairs they used to use to watch tennis being played. Uncomfortable looking things. Must have been hard to get out of."

"I don't mind what's there as long as there are no rats," Chloe said with a shudder.

"Hardly likely — they would've gnawed their way out long since. Don't say anything to the Reverend Joshua or he'll be stripping off that paper tonight. He said to me last week that it was too bad there were no exciting discoveries about the house they are going to have."

"Well, I hope there's something to interest him though I won't tell him till we've got it open. I can imagine the cobwebs and dust. Before you start I'll take this canvas into Dane's study. I'm doing it for there. A surprise for him. He gave me that book to read on the Port Hills by Gordon Ogilvie. Marvellous book. I was fascinated to see photographs of some of the places Captain Scott knew and loved . . . Joseph Kinsey's Clifton garden, near Sumner on the other side of the hills, for instance. And Captain Scott in the *Terra Nova* garden party in 1910, with the great explorer distinguished in the company by a handkerchief in his hand and a November entry in his diary, calling it an enchanted place and recording how they had slept in the garden under peaceful clear skies. He spoke of a sunny corner there blazing with masses of red and golden flowers." She had those colours dominating the canvas. A labour of love.

She showed the photo to Barry. He said, "What a great girl you are. I had no interest in the local history till I started this job and now Monica says I can talk of nothing else. Just imagine if we found one of Captain Scott's old dog sledges stowed away there. Canterbury Museum would fall on our necks with joy."

She laughed and picked up her materials and took them down to Dane's study. Despite her embargo on telling Joshua, that evening she couldn't help imagining things of interest under those stairs, perhaps old records or diaries.

All of a sudden Abbie looked up from her book and asked, "How's Barry getting on with the papering?"

Chloe replied, "Very well — it's made it much lighter. I love my little cubbyhole. Whenever I need fresh air I go up to the tower. Barry told me it used to be called the 'Admiral's Tower' — quite fascinating. Isn't cubbyhole a funny word? I wonder when it was invented and why it was called that?"

"Only one way to find out," said Abbie. She leaned forward and drew out a shabby dictionary from the bookcase near her. "When I was teaching I always taught my pupils that the moment they came across a word new to them it was a golden rule to look it up and use it."

"Once a teacher, always a teacher," approved Joshua. "It's my turn to make our last cuppa so I'd better not dodge it. Anyone want cheese on toast?"

They both did and he departed kitchen-wards.

Abbie found the place in the dictionary. "It's got rather a nice meaning. It says here: 'a cubby hole . . . a snug enclosed space'."

"That's how I feel about it. A little refuge where I can sketch and dream."

"Somebody else found it a refuge long ago," said Abbie. "Dane's grandmother on his father's side told me years ago it was called 'Verena's cubbyhole'. Perhaps when she was fighting her nostalgia for things known and familiar, she'd go there to weep and ease the pain. Or perhaps to see some ship slipping out between the heads and wish she was on it. Poor girl. Poor girl. Perhaps her violin playing eased the ache."

Chloe had dropped her book. She bent forward and retrieved it, and, avoiding direct gaze at Abbie, said, "Verena? What an unusual name."

"Yes, but pretty isn't it? One of Georgette Heyer's books has a Verena in it. A minor character. Let me see, which was it? Oh yes, it's Sylvester, one of my favourites."

They didn't linger too long over their tea. Chloe yawned. "Well, I'm for bed. Nothing like sea air to make you sleepy. Goodnight all."

When she reached the haven of her own room she stared at her reflection in the mirror unbelievingly. She knew she was in a state of semi-shock. Yes, it was an unusual name. It was her own second name and she had been named after Great-Granny. No wonder she had called her Greeny. Children just starting to talk found Vs very difficult.

Realisation was dawning on her. Gran must've known this was where those sketches had been done; have known those Maori artefacts had been brought by Verena when she left Gregory and returned to the scenes of her girlhood. Gran's reticence accounted for some of it, of course. She'd said once, "She was a wonderful person and a great example to all who knew her. She'd had a sad life but didn't let it ruin her later years," and Chloe hadn't felt she could probe.

But coming to grips with the idea that this was why Gran had been so keen for her to come to New Zealand, was a most un-welcome thought . . . Dane could be furious. He would think she had known and had let him go off on a wild-goose chase. She told herself that the trip was partly a business trip . . . but there were thousands of dollars involved, a heavy expense on top of all the restoration on Inglethorpe House, for a return flight.

She didn't sleep well. The sound of high tide disturbed her tonight. Usually it acted like a lullaby. But tonight she knew beyond any doubt that the sands the tide was breaking on were what Verena, in the bitterness of grief and guilt had written of. The starfish, the sea horses . . . this was her far-flung shore. If only Gran had told them that first happy day when Dane had come into the shop. If only she herself had probed into her family history.

Perhaps she might have guessed had it not been for the sketches of Kaikoura and Cheviot and Picton. And of Christchurch. She'd felt the artist might have lived there or at least made a long stay there.

In all it was a night that seemed interminable, but she must appear normal in front of Abbie and Josh. It wasn't really successful, for when she came back from her room after breakfast, clad in denim overalls with braces over the shoulders, she heard Joshua say: "I thought the same. Looked very washed out. But I expect she's missing Dane. It will seem dull with him away all this time and just us two old fogeys to live with."

Abbie agreed. "I expect that's it. I remember well how churned up I was all those years ago, love, when you went home to New Zealand. Edinburgh seemed a desert. That day when I went down to Waverley Station to meet you I was terribly afraid you might have changed, even that you might have met again some girl from your earlier days. Then you came to me by the bookstall, caught me up and said, 'I know this is no place to propose but I can't take on this parish in North Canterbury unless you come too, as my wife.' Oh, Joshua, all my doubts fled."

Chloe had the door open a crack so saw Joshua bend down and kiss Abbie, a kiss that was anything but a peck, and she envied her. She waited a moment before entering. "Well, it's me for the dusters and scrubbing brush this morning my dears. Barry and I are going to go on with the stripping." She didn't mention the concealed cupboard, or their curiosity would make them want to help and they'd have a sense of anticlimax when they discovered it was, as Barry predicted, just full of discarded chairs and other junk. Not to mention the spiders and cobwebs.

And it was. She and Barry regarded each other with dismay and disappointment, then he laughed. "Despite my prediction I still hoped we might find some valuable old ornament or even some mahogany chest of drawers just wanting polishing."

She made her tone light. "Yes, or even some linen, convent-made, or old horse-brasses which would have delighted Sarah."

They heard Joshua calling from below, "Barry, you're wanted at Inglethorpe House. Phyl's had another idea! She says it'll take only an hour or two."

Barry groaned but said, "Right, I'll come," then to Chloe, "leave that till I get back, it's filthy."

But of course she couldn't. At least she could get at that conglomeration of old cases, chairs with broken legs, worn mats from a day long distant. She was soon as dusty as the relics. Then she spied something that looked more hopeful, a tarnished picture frame, stacked under some old window-blinds. Wouldn't Barry be over the moon if she unearthed some colonial treasure, say one of Goldie's famous pictures of historic and handsome Maoris? She pulled it out carefully, not to damage the canvas; valuable or not someone had painted it so it deserved to be handled carefully. The next moment she was gazing, astounded, at the finished picture of the sketch she had copied that mural from for the window display . . . the deserted village, beautifully executed in oils. One part of her awareness appreciated this, but her attention was riveted upon the signature in the right-hand corner. A bald signature, there was no chance of it being mistaken for anything else . . . Verena Inglethorpe. No date. The frame, a gilt one, was tarnished. She picked up her feather duster, brushed it with the lightest of touches, and took it over to her drawing table.

This confirmed her realisation of last night. This was the unhappy Verena, whose descendants Dane was trying to trace. And he wasn't going to like any of this. Vaguely she wondered why Verena hadn't taken this with her. After all, she'd managed to take the sketches, the artefacts. But perhaps she'd thought the frame too bulky.

She moved the balance of the stuff more carefully. Just as well. She unearthed another picture. Also signed Verena Inglethorpe. On the back it said, 'Self portrait of the artist'. She studied it carefully. Yes, even in these young features she could trace those she remembered of Greeny: the slightly aquiline nose, the oval face, the dented chin. But this was a lovely, happy young girl. Disillusionment must have come later. Chloe's eyes filled with tears . . . and not only disillusionment, but the guilt Verena had known, the rue and remorse, she had suffered. Chloe picked up some paper discarded from the rolls of wallpaper and wrapped them up, then went down one flight to her bedroom. She put them in her wardrobe behind her hanging dresses. She wasn't going to show them to anyone yet.

She sorted out the rest of the stuff before calling Joshua and Abbie to show them the cupboard. She said, indicating her drawing-table piled high, "Not exciting stuff, in fact the only thing to thrill Barry was the door itself. Fine kauri he said, once he gets the layers of paper off."

Joshua loved it too, and Abbie pounced on some tarnished curtain rings. "Just right for our archway in the hall over there." It was such a little thing but Chloe suffered a pang. These two dear people had counted unhatched chickens too soon. They'd made up their minds that Dane's attraction was serious. But what would happen when Dane realised Gran knew where those sketches had been drawn and was bound to leap to the conclusion Chloe had known too? It could kill any feeling he had for Chloe stone dead. He could despise her for being so deceitful. Josh and Abbie would be disappointed in her too, to say nothing of Phyl and Ross. Well, she'd have to just sit it out till Dane returned.

She had counted on getting letters from Dane; as an author he'd write marvellous letters she was sure. There weren't any. Just postcards to the entire family, addressed to his uncle Joshua. Abbie seemed to have expected letters too. She said, with a sigh as one arrived, "Well, at least it's an outsized one, but . . ."

Joshua read it aloud. It had been hectic, Dane said. Mostly re the TV series. Rewarding though. Better to be on the spot. Now he was up north. Had gone as far as Burghead for the purpose of gathering gen for the book after the current one. He was having a link in it with the Viking attacks of long ago, and had seen the very place where they had landed. He'd also done some research in Northumberland, rather fruitlessly. Chloe knew an immense relief. If it was fruitless it would at least give her a chance to explain that she had no idea when she took this on that Greeny had ever been here, that she was the Verena whose second husband had always called her Renie, that her name in her second marriage had been MacAlpine. That much at least Chloe had now pieced together and he must *please* believe she hadn't known. Much better to confess it than to have had him find out. Confess? Well, at least be able to tell him face to face. Not have him discover it from some long-ago marriage certificate. Chloe stopped worrying, though she did wonder he hadn't written a letter, just to her . . . a love letter in which perhaps he'd get carried away and reveal more of his own feelings. There were times when she wondered if she should phone Gran and ask her to tell Dane. It would be wonderful not to have to explain it when he came back. But would Leonora get Dane to understand she had merely had a wish for Chloe to see Hauroko Bay where Verena had spent some unhappy years and had acted so badly? Nevertheless, Chloe found herself hoping passionately that Verena had also known hours of happiness, and that there might have been some of remembered sweetness in their few days of reunited bonding that might have lessened her remorse. In the end Chloe decided it would be cowardly to ask Leonora to tell Dane.

To fill in the hours when she wasn't busy helping Barry, she decided she must do what she had promised Dane — look up some data he'd gathered in his earlier visit; also for the book after his current one. This had intrigued Chloe. She'd always imagined authors as so possessed, so engrossed with the current book that they wouldn't think about the one to come till this one was finished and the last words to solve the mystery were there above 'The End'. No so. Dane had told of "The need to express myself in another story!" Well, it was odd, but seeing he'd given up so much to launch this project for Phyl and Ross, it was over to her to have these notes found and checked.

The moment she entered his study she felt close to him. Of *course* he'd understand. Of *course* he was sincere in those more tender moments. She sat down in his chair, lost in remembrance. That idyllic one standing in the sea, the shallow waves washing against their bare feet, the feel of the live sea horse in her hand, Dane carefully depositing it where it wouldn't be stranded. Not just a kiss he had said but a commitment; the sharing of that moment when the lark sang in the sky, and his stirring words about feeling a sense of kinship with all who had ever lain upon a hill and listened to a lark. She felt comforted by all this. Surely it added up to the sort of bond she so desired? She was making a mountain out of the proverbial molehill. Dane might just dismiss it as an odd secrecy of her grandmother.

She set to work and a sort of ease descended upon her. It was quite a task, much larger than she had imagined. There were umpteen notebooks of the type he had described. It was made a little easier by the fact he had carefully dated the time and place where he had written these items.

She found what he had wanted, and smiled to see that it was headed: 'Burghead on the Moray Firth'. Now he was back there garnering more facts. Evidently at first it had been just the germ of an idea. It was intriguing too, simply said: 'Have a long-ago forebear of the hero come out to Dunedine in NZ with the Scots settlers who left there with the Rev. Thomas Burns, nephew of the famous Robbie, to found a mainly Presbyterian colony, where more freedom of conscience was allowed — this after the Disruption. They came in 1848, two years before the Anglican one in 1850. My idea is too vague yet, but possibly a present-day descendant goes home to Scotland, visits his ancestral home and finds an old legend about treasure being hidden when the Danes descended upon them.'

That was all, but Chloe's imagination was caught and fired by it, and her recent worries receded in importance. Her mind began toying with suitable titles. Rather a cheek — she supposed authors knew from the start — but wouldn't it be wonderful if she was ever asked to suggest one. It acted on her spirits, like magic. Dane had added, later, because that was dated too, 'Have a Scots heroine frustrate him at first in his search. Pick a suitable name. Possibly a red-headed one, not afraid to speak her mind. He falls madly in love with her but wishes they weren't opponents in this. No idea how it can be resolved; he also wonders if he can — in the language of the long-ago — lay siege to her heart, and enough to make her face the uprooting to another hemisphere. Possibly called *Conflict of Loyalties*.'

Abbie called her to lunch and when she saw that Chloe's appetite did full justice to the tender lamb chops cooked with rosemary, and the stuffed tomatoes, put it down to the more intimate hours of working in Dane's study, and the fact that his return wasn't so far away now.

"Did you find what he wanted you to look up?"

Chloe nodded. "And found it fascinating, to say nothing of wishing the story was written so I could read it."

"Well," said Abbie contentedly, "you'll probably be able to before anyone else. Not that, as a rule, he cares for anyone to read his books until they are in print, but I imagine that won't apply to you seeing he asked you to look those notes up for him. In that, too, he's usually averse to anyone horning in. Says once you admit anyone into your thought processes the story no longer clamours to be written. Odd, isn't it? It will, however, I imagine, make you feel part of the story long before it reaches Miles Burford."

Abbie said no more, due Chloe suspected, to Joshua directing a warning glance across the table at her. She supposed he didn't want her to overdo. Nevertheless it gave Chloe an inward glow. It had been a wonderful morning. The items read had given her the most endearing glimpses into Dane's mind, especially the extracts from poems, long-loved poems, to be used in some future story as yet unborn. Of *course* he'd be understanding about this — a minor problem compared with some his characters had to wrestle with.

As she rose Joshua said, "I'll help with the dishes — off you go to your happy hunting. You may find he's added to his nucleus a bit further on. I know that's his custom. He broods upon each story long after the first inspiration till it takes a hold on him, and if you do find further references it would help him greatly to have them co-ordinated. Especially when he's lost so much time this year."

As Chloe departed full of contentment and anticipation Abbie told her, "Elizabeth Ffoulkes rang up to say someone she knows has unearthed a 1920s dress for you to wear at that re-enactment of the dances of that time for this ball Doctor and Innis are giving for their daughter's coming-of-age. Elizabeth says it should suit you — a deep green like your eyes. I'm so thrilled they're having it here. It has delighted Phyl. It'll be well written up in the *Argus*, that's for sure, with Elizabeth doing it."

"It's so good of them to ask me — the stranger in your midst — but I've never tried to do some of those dances."

"Not a stranger now," said Joshua, "but one of us, and you'll soon master them if you get a bit of practice."

Abbie's tone was shrewd. "What he means is that he'd like to coach you. Because when all her family were home, his mother showed them how to perform. He's an expert at the slow foxtrot and the Charleston even. Possibly the tango too, or am I out in my dates, Joshua?"

He smiled at his wife affectionately. "Possibly you are — but I daresay they won't stick too closely to accuracy. And for Innis's sake, whose idea this was, I hope the young fry enjoy seeing the old ones make fools of themselves! But if I can achieve partners as lovely as Chloe I shan't complain. Poor Chloe — she's looking astonished at the idea of an elderly clergyman doing the Charleston! But I wasn't always a man of the cloth, and I had a very young-hearted mother."

"Just as well," remarked Abbie. "Dear Lucy — if she hadn't brought Joshua up the way she did I'd never have married him. You can't imagine me wed to a narrow, hidebound sort of parson, can you?"

Joshua groaned. "If I were you I'd be off to the study right now, dear child, before my wife gives you any examples of things that prove I wasn't at all stiff and starchy — I'll wish you happy hunting, love."

As Chloe passed his chair she dropped an

affectionate kiss upon his head. "You are both darlings," she said.

An hour later Chloe knew that, while it was hunting, it wasn't happy.

She had, as had been predicted, found a further reference to the Burghead inspiration, that had delighted her, but then she spied another similar notebook. At first the date on the first page interested her, as she realised it continued on from the last entry of the previous one which meant it was just before she and Dane met. She enjoyed the humorous word-sketches of the signing sessions from the Highlands down, and her pulses quickened as she found him nearing Haslemere. He'd used this one as a trip record as well as a jotter for his work. She read: 'Now to completely relax. Thank heaven I've a link with home because of Victoria Doig.'

She turned the page, took in much of it at a glance, then stared at it unbelievingly . . .

She couldn't *not* recognise it — there it was, word for word; Hudson's actual proposal was missing, that was all. She burned with indignation as she read. For anyone to eavesdrop, however unwittingly, and to copy it down was the ultimate in — in — what

236

was the word she wanted? Unchivalrousness to say the least — in fact, to use an old-fashioned word — caddishness!

She turned the page and a further enormity was revealed. The next day's entry: 'I can't believe my incredible luck! How many authors have a character and the nucleus of a plot handed to them on a platter? Good job I had a glimpse of that high-spirited redhead as she flashed by. I'd already toyed with the idea of using the incident — but not the details or setting — but to have her suddenly revealed as Leonora's granddaughter was a gift from the gods — someone who already had an interest in the bay, who was intrigued by the deserted village, who rattled off Goldsmith's poem at the drop of a hat; and an interior decorator to boot! Woke up at three in the morning and jotted this down.

'I already had my hero — much more interested in solving the mystery than in his love life. But here was the answer and just what Miles wanted. I would have her disturbing him greatly, putting him off the job in hand, but then the great idea was born. Have the girl put off men for a bit. She is an idealist — bring Shakespeare's sonnets in — wants to be wooed as in the days of old. Along comes the hero . . . seemingly her ideal man. The complete antithesis to Hudson. Hero decides on an experiment . . . will she fall immediately for romantic speeches? For a moon-track shining along a deserted shore, waves creaming back, a rose garden, the scent of rosemary and lavender! . . . Speeches laden with meaning and romance? Must see more of her. Thank goodness still some time left. I'll give it a go.'

Give it a go! And she had fallen for it hook, line and sinker! *Or so he thought.* Just wait till he got back, the cold-blooded schemer! She'd turn the tables.

The hot thoughts tumbled through her mind. She would show him! Two could play at that game. She'd lead him on, then laugh at him; and at some dramatic moment when he thought he knew how his heroine would react, she'd reveal *he'd* been made a fool of — not her! And the more she led him on, the greater fool he'd feel. It would turn his character drawing topsy-turvy.

Oh, Chloe might have been in a fine rage when Hudson proposed in a crowded tearoom, in so prosaic a manner and got his comeuppance, but it was nothing to the rage that possessed her now. She supposed it was because *this* time her heart was involved. She burned as she recalled how she had responded to his kisses, to his beautifully worded compliments, to his every touch, to his endearments. She had sometimes even lain awake savouring them, reading more into them than had been meant. She was just an experimental subject. How infatuation could blind you to reality . . . but not any more. Oh no, Dane Inglethorpe had a bewildering experience ahead of him. And when he reached the ultimate, finding he didn't know his heroine at all, she hoped it would turn his labours into ashes. Perhaps into ashes literally — he wouldn't be able to have his heroine continue as he had imagined her, not the fool he'd thought her. Not deceived by a charm of manner, but all the time laughing at him behind his back and encouraging him on to further insincere behaviour.

She sat on, planning it, her bitterness of heart turning all the sweetness to acid, the warmth of love to a deadly chilliness, all her dreams to dust. Who was it that said: 'Tread softly for you tread on my dreams'? Well, she'd awakened from dreaming. She hoped that in due time *he* would feel as foolish as *she* felt.

What had he said one day when she had answered him cheekily, laughingly, "Oh girl, no one would ever get the better of you! No wonder I feel Miles is going to say 'Well, my suggestion to pep up the love interest has certainly borne fruit'." And it will have done, more than *he* ever dreamed.

Suddenly she realised *she* could read how he had handled it. It would give her ideas how to treat it. She rose, went across to the seven-drawer file where he put his manuscript every night in case of fire. The disks too. She pulled at the top handle . . . it was locked. She forgot about the fire precautions, thought instead: He dare not risk my seeing it. Well, so much the easier to lead him on.

She went back to his desk, stared through the window unseeingly at the lovely emerald waters — could this be *her* thinking vengeful thoughts like these?

Then she put her head on the blotter, where in his first jottings he must have hatched this diabolical scheme, nurturing it from those first damning lines, and remembered how he had said, on the plane, that he was dying to get home so he could enlarge on an inspiration that had flashed upon him shortly after finishing the signing sessions.

It was then that Chloe wept.

Chapter Nine

Sometimes her thoughts played traitor to her. She didn't want the intensity of her emotions to cool down but she must — if she was to treat Dane as he so richly deserved — maintain the temperature and not succumb to his charm; that charm that had caused him to play fast and loose with her feelings.

It was inevitable that Joshua and Abbie should notice her mood, but maddening that they were putting it down to missing Dane. They were spending more and more hours at their house. It was realising a dream for them. She was almost moved to tears the day they arrived back from the city with a plaque in wood, beautifully executed, a nameplate for their white picket fence. It said 'Avalon'. She thought for a moment then it clicked, and she said rather unsteadily because the landscape was wavering and dancing before her, "Of course — Tennyson's 'Island-valley of Avilion':

'Where falls not hail, or rain or any snow,

Nor ever wind blows loudly; but it lies
Deep-meadow'd, happy, fair with orchard
   lawns
And bowery hollows crown'd with summer
   sea
Where I will heal me of my grievous
   wound.' "

Abbie said: "I've never regretted being a minister's wife because of Joshua and all he's brought me throughout the years — the riches of the mind and treasures of the heart — but at times I did kick against the pricks. The Vestry's taste in carpet wasn't always mine; sometimes we had great draughty barns of places, or small modern ones that rather skimped the space our sons and daughters needed in their teenage years, so this is a dream come true — the views, the sense of anchoring, the permanence of knowing you'll see the trees and vines you plant reaching maturity; in fact the sense of *this is ours*."

How Chloe loved them both, the bond between them, the unembarrassed way they revealed those feelings; the fun, the shared laughter, their occasional spats that made them human . . . and they were counting on a marriage between her and Dane to free them to realise it all. Oh why couldn't it have gone that way? But she'd been a fool, allowing herself to be duped into thinking it was for real! At the moment she couldn't bear to think of their disappointment. She had no idea of how they would react. It was like depriving a child of its much-loved teddy bear.

Just as well she got involved in the preparations for the ball; all her artistic skills brought into play for the decorations. They'd found a multitude of old ornaments stacked away in a lumber room at the top of the house, so much of it fitting to the occasion, because in addition to the Victorian bric-a-brac of Aubrey and Caroline's day, all generations were represented — even to the Art Deco items of the 1920s and 30s. Hilary spent hours over here, driving over from Harvest Moon Bay. She'd followed in her parents' footsteps and was a nurse at the Cherrington Inlet Hospital and she and the whole staff were delighted with it all. "Like living in a different world," Hilary exulted.

They were enamoured of Chloe's frock. The sea-green, the shimmer of the silk, the low-cut square neck. But Chloe wished Phyl hadn't said, "And of course the greenstone *tiki* my brother gave Chloe for Christmas will be ideal with it." Chloe said she thought a rope of beads would be more in keeping with the era, but Phyl cried out against that. "But it's just right and coming from the other side of the world you probably don't realise that *tiki*s were never out of fashion from pre-*pakeha* days on. None of our portraits of lovely Maori maidens would be the same without their green *tiki*s against their golden-brown skins." Chloe gave in. She wasn't proof against the enthusiasm of this family she loved so well. At least, all except Dane, she hastily amended in her thoughts. A stressful time lay ahead of her, so she'd jolly well enjoy this dance as much as she could.

At last the great day came. The dinner beforehand was superb — couldn't help but be with Phyl, not only planning the courses, but working sheer wizardry in the kitchen. Then the ball, with no canned music! This was drifting out into the lovely summer air with harmonious sounds, stirringly romantic, the big French windows open to the garden with its perfume of roses and cinnamon pinks, lavender and rosemary. It was rewarding to see the delight of the young ones, caught up in the spirit of the occasion. It was like a fairy tale when those invited for the dance — the dinner had been for family and close friends — began arriving from Lyttelton and all the bays of the harbour on both sides, by boat, singing the songs of the 1920s as they came, young and old alike.

"Truly songs upon the wind," commented Ross. "Just look at my own grandparents and the others of their generation — they are combining sheer pleasure with a certain amount of nostalgia." The old tunes, 'Moonlight and Roses', 'Weeping Willow Lane' and 'I'll be Loving you — Always' didn't seem incongruous at all, and the young ones had practised well, thought Chloe as Joshua foxtrotted her round the floor. If only she could keep her mind from dwelling on the fact of how wonderful it might have been had she never read those entries in the jotter — if Dane had been the romantic and chivalrous figure she had taken him for, if he had been here, waltzing with her, instead of Ross, if only . . . if only . . . Oh, what was the use?

There was a sudden stir at the wide-flung doors and Merle Nathan was framed in the space, and with her someone who could only be Roderick Ffoulkes, he was so like Jeremy, his father. The music stopped, there was a cry of "Surprise! Surprise!" and "Here the conquering hero comes . . . back from the jungle", and a surge towards them.

Then Chloe saw him. Dane — two days early! The three of them had had time to change but Chloe had eyes only for Dane — she'd not seen him in formal dress before. What magnificent shoulders. What clean-cut masculine attractiveness.

Their eyes met and all the icy disdain and planned reception of him Chloe had looked forward to, fled from mind and heart. The setting was so different from what she had imagined, undermined with a sort of romantic aura. And no one would have taken the look in his eyes for anything other than admiration and gladness. He came across to her, his eyes taking in the perfect match of her eyes and the low-waisted frock, the carving of the *tiki*. Ross turned away, spoke to someone else, and Dane came swiftly to her side.

"I had the incredible luck to get a cancelled seat on the same plane with Merle and Roddy. Merle had phoned her father and when I heard what was on, I was determined to be with you."

Chloe wished all the guests could fade away, and she could summon up every anti-feeling she had been nurturing. This wasn't fair, an atmosphere like this. She swallowed, said in a normal voice, "You must go and greet Andrew and Innis and

Hilary. See you later."

"Not if I know it," he declared. "Look, the orchestra is having a break — come with me, and the next dance is mine." He took her arm and steered her through the crowd.

Greetings and interval over, they drifted into a slow foxtrot. There was just nothing else Chloe could do. She said, rather inanely she thought, "I see you must have benefited by your grandmother's coaching as well as Joshua did."

He laughed. "I bet Gran is watching us and thinking, 'If I'd planned it, it couldn't be more ideal'," and he exchanged a smile with his grandparents on the floor.

Bemused, Chloe, drifting slowly in his arms, thought there was something to be said for these old steps.

Several dances later, he separated her from the throng. "Getting too hot — come on outside. Pity to waste a night like this indoors, don't you think?"

It was much too sudden, his appearance, to summon her wits and begin to treat him as he so richly deserved. He knew the layout of the garden so well, and adroitly steered her into the shrubbery where little paths ran between rhododendrons of all colours, not quite past their best, treading on a carpet of dying white snowball petals beneath the guelders and the pink of the early roses.

He paused on a little circular lawn in the midst of it, and turned her to face him. "Much better — all I hoped for. Chloe, did you ever see such a sky? Look up." She looked up at the magnificence of dark blue, lit by a myriad stars, caught in the beauty of it.

"Know W.B. Yeats at all, Chloe?" Dane asked her, but didn't wait for her to answer. "This is exactly the night he wrote about, don't you think? Listen:

'Had I the heavens' embroidered
    cloths,
Enwrought with golden and silver
    lights,
The blue and the dim and the dark
    cloths
Of night, and light and the half-light,
I would spread the cloth under your
    feet:
But I, being poor, have only my
    dreams;
I have spread my dreams under your
    feet;
Tread softly because you tread on my
    dreams.' "

Chloe caught her breath, knew joy and pain intermingled, told herself this didn't mean a thing. It was the author in him not the lover. Well, he'd not find any reaction in her, no racing pulses.

But those pulses betrayed her. There could be only one end to a moment like this . . . he bent that handsome head of his and kissed her. The gold and silver lights seemed to swing above her. She despised herself as she kissed him back.

He said, holding her closer, "What are you shivering for, Chloe?"

What could she say? Not the truth. Because this is sheer ecstasy, that's why. Because I know you for what you are! A gay deceiver. Because to you I'm just copy! The subject of your experiment. All calculated to give you what you wanted for the love interest in your book. And heaven help me — even now I'm falling for what seems like sincerity. But just wait!

Chloe knew it was stupid but she told herself that one night pretending all was well couldn't matter. After tonight she would disillusion him, make him unsure of himself, begin to think she had just played with him, that this was only an interlude, and her real world was in the northern hemisphere.

They took Lucy and Stephen back to Headland House, of course, when all the revelry was done. Dane said, "The years between that time and now, slipped away. It's not given to everyone to relive the past. Somehow tonight I had this strange longing for everyone to have had dreams realised as we have had. I thought that if Gregory had only realised Verena needed a party, a ball, now and then — if he had been more gifted with words, there need never have been that tragedy in their lives. Oh, I know it's long ago, but tonight Chloe in that dress reminded me of that old self-portrait of Verena that used to be kicking around here, in her green frock with her *tiki* below her throat. What happened to it?"

Chloe felt her cheeks burn. Dane continued. "I was just a little boy the only time I ever saw it. Can't even remember whether it was here or over at Inglethorpe. A pity, because young as I was, I seem to remember it was well done. I have an impression of everything green — perhaps *her* eyes were green too." He looked at Chloe and she hoped he wouldn't ask why she was blushing. What she would do with the portrait when she left in the not-too-far distant future she knew not. Without a doubt it belonged here but wouldn't it be equally at home in Leonora's New Zealand room, reunited with those sketches and artefacts Gran treasured so because of the warmth of love and homelife Verena and Big Granddad had given to a bewildered orphaned child?

Lucy Winchmore said: "When I first saw Chloe I noticed her eyes and decided perhaps there was something to reincarnation after all."

Chloe looked up to see Dane's gaze upon her. She said hurriedly, "Look, the sky is growing light and the stars are fading one by one, and if Dane hasn't got jet lag, he ought to have."

They went to bed and not a single alarm clock was set.

Dane was plunged into gruelling work at his desk barely two days later. He had to go into details about the TV series not dreamed of when he first conceived the tale, or had thought of when revisions were done. He had a tentative deadline to submit the current book and what he called stock-and-station business, delayed while he was away, could be delayed no longer. His mail was heavy — most gratifying of course to read of how much joy readers had experienced in his books, but no time to answer them as deserved because they were inspiring. The best he could do was send acknowledgement cards.

There was no way Chloe could begin to make him realise she had seen through him, in fact had read his cold-blooded plan to use her as a guinea pig. She had despised herself the morning after the ball for falling for his facile charm, that veneer of easy speech and undoubted physical magnetism. It hadn't helped one bit when Abbie the next night, played some of the romantic songs of the 1920s, because Stephen and Lucy were in a mood of nostalgia. They had sung along:

'After the ball is over, after the break of
    morn;
After the dancers leaving, after the stars
    are gone,
Many a heart is aching if you could read
    them all,
Many the hopes that have vanished after
    the ball.'

It had been irritating to see Dane sitting there, joining in now and then in some remembered tune, to the delight of his grandparents. He had been giving them a rare evening at the bay and being maddeningly casual about it. Little did he guess what was coming to him. Chloe gritted her teeth at the necessity for holding back on what she intended to do, but she didn't want her plan to be sandwiched in between faxes and overseas phonecalls and that stack of mail. So his absorption in his work, his correspondence, the few hours he could manage to tear himself away from it for urgent matters on the estate, was a barrier.

Joshua and Abbie seemed engrossed in their garden in that village row. All the colours of late summer bloomed and the perfumes of the second chapter of roses climbing over arches and trellises; aubretia and campanulas spilling bluely over the rocks that had been upthrust since that volcano aeons ago; nasturtiums in all their glorious golds and reds, geraniums that grew so well here and never needed to be brought indoors in winter she was told, blazed against the stone walls of the old house; wallflowers and forget-me-nots vied for a place in the herbaceous borders, the crepe myrtles crowned their branches with rose and mauve and apples were reddening on the boughs.

Chloe somehow disciplined herself to biding her time and doing all Dane requested of her, looking up quotations, checking long-ago dates of the Vikings' invasions, times and seasons. If only she could have attributed this to him wanting her to prolong her stay — in fact, never to leave here — but he was just making a convenience of her. He had approved the redecoration of the cubbyhole, been mildly interested when Barry went on about restoring the kauri door in devoted French polishing, said abstractedly, "Pity you hadn't discovered some valuable heirloom but I suppose it was just junk."

"Sure was," said Barry, "you should've seen it — deckchairs with rotting canvas that would have split the moment anyone attempted to sit in them, old pans and saucepans, even a few handleless cups — they must all have been hoarders, generation after generation."

Dane nodded. "They were. Those old barns and sheds were once testimony to that. Dad had some grand bonfires when he took over, thank goodness." He looked at Chloe, busy at her worktable. "I guess, seeing you're history mad, you hoped for old diaries. Would have been marvellous had you discovered one of Goldie's Maori studies, or Charles Lindaeur's scenes."

Chloe shrugged, "Well it was hardly in *my* interests. Not my particular sphere. Not like discovering a Renoir or a Rembrandt."

He looked at her sharply. "How snooty can you get? Yet earlier you were revelling in the fact that our history was so young."

Barry said hastily, much in the manner of a grown-up trying to divert quarrelling children, "Well, boss, mustn't hold you up any more or you won't have the brass to pay for all this. They tell me you've been bogged down ever since you got home. Beggared if I ever thought producing books was so much hard labour."

"It certainly is, but against the hours of sheer toil there are the moments of inspiration that make up for it all, the occasional flashes of the germ of an idea that hits you in the midriff and sends you scurrying for notebook and ballpoint!"

Chloe bit back the words she wanted to utter. How satisfying to have been able to say: "Like listening in to a private conversation in a Surrey village for instance and feeling you've been handed a ready-made plot on a platter. But perhaps not entirely ready-made. *You* had to help it along, make a psychological study of it, no matter whose feelings were bruised on the way." It would have been a golden opportunity, but Barry had to be there!

Abbie hadn't appeared to notice anything

which was a blessing. With her matchmaking slant, it could have been very alarming. Especially as it was in their interest.

Till now Chloe hadn't bothered to take the days off she was entitled to. Earlier she had said, "But every day's a holiday in this delectable spot", but not any longer!

Dane, this day, had departed for his study as soon as lunch was finished. Chloe dressed very carefully. This was to be her afternoon and evening in Christchurch. She'd been gone half an hour when Dane emerged and asked, "Where's Chloe? I want her to look up some architectural details for me. It's just possible she'll know this period or at least what book to look it up in, and we could go over to Canterbury Public Library, and if they haven't got it, they would order it for me."

Abbie said dryly, "I'm afraid someone else had an idea she might be interested in architecture, only nothing as ancient as you evidently have in mind. He called for her not long ago though I had offered her our car. But he turned that down and who could blame him — the chance of having a looker like Chloe to himself for much longer."

Dane looked thunderous. "Blast it! I suppose this means she'll be out all afternoon."

Abbie observed comfortably, "Oh much

longer than that, dear boy, he's giving her dinner at Noah's and taking her to a Gilbert and Sullivan operetta afterwards. One of the reasons he didn't want her taking our car — said he didn't like the idea of a girl driving back over the hills and round the bays in the dark."

Dane scowled. "Who is *he?* And where did she get to know him? Some retired architect interested in her work, I suppose?"

"Dear me, no." Abbie's voice was as smooth as cream. She was glad Joshua was over in the new garden. He'd have been suspicious. She continued, "He'd be younger than you. Nearer her age. It's Clive Douglasson, one of our up-and-coming professional men, with his speciality restoration of some of our pioneer homes. So of course he's most interested in Chloe and wanted to show her some of our early colonial gems. He was here a lot while you were away, and was at the ball too, but he left before you arrived because he had his mother there. She wanted to meet Chloe, of course, but didn't want to be there till the small hours of the morning. She's not a dancer, though for sure Clive is."

Dane went on scowling, then said, "I'll ring up the library and see if they have anything they can recommend."

Abbie commented innocently, "Why, I thought that book wasn't started yet."

He looked at her indignantly. "You know very well I do a lot of research long before I start each story. You can't just start with the bare bones of it. You need to ponder and ponder on it."

"Like a broody hen," said Abbie, "and now I'm off to join Josh."

It was very late when Clive brought her home. She came in laughing and flushed, in an aquamarine frock and with the same colour repeated in the *paua* shell earrings Abbie and Josh had given her for Christmas, swinging from her ears.

Dane was still in the sitting-room. Clive followed Chloe in as she greeted him. "Oh hello — didn't expect you'd be up still."

He'd stopped scowling but said coolly, "On hills like ours I like to know everyone's safe home."

She grinned. "At one stage we thought we wouldn't be. We stopped outside the Sign of the Kiwi — for the view — and Clive's car wouldn't start again. I was mean enough to enjoy the fact that even cars like Clive's can be temperamental, like my shabby old car back home, but on no account will I allow him to drive back at this hour. Abbie always has the spare bed made up, so he's going to stay the night. It will give me peace of mind. We're starving now so I'll do cheese and bacon strips and a pot of coffee."

Dane leapt up. "I'll do it, and wash our mugs up after so you can get straight off to bed afterwards, Clive." So he wasn't going to leave them together! Chloe was amused. This was something she hadn't counted on but it couldn't be better. No one would think Chloe and Clive had had a full day the way they chatted on, with those green eyes sparkling.

"It's been marvellous. If ever I do any articles on this — there's a local paper back home I've done a few for — illustrated with sketches, these Colonial styles would add variety. And Clive is going to lend me some of the notes he took when studying for his degree. Though I value even more his maturer knowledge gained through personal experience. There were some old pioneer houses I was just itching to sketch."

Dane said, though not rudely, "Hasn't that subject been done to death? There was a sort of renaissance of it for the one hundred and twenty-fifth anniversary. It'll be revived with later milestones, for sure, but I doubt if there are any more architectural gems to be discovered."

Chloe disagreed. "Some we saw today have never been featured yet. Jeremy Ffoulkes is interested in doing a series for his paper, later to be produced as a book. We called in to the *Argus* and he took us to tea. Dane, there are some splendid old houses in Merivale and Fendalton and on the lower slopes of the Cashmeres. Quite different from here too."

Clive said: "But while you were away I took lots of notes. Phyl seemed pleased."

"Well, she would be wouldn't she? All free advertising. Like me, all is grist to the mill as Chloe so often reminds me. I'll ring a garage this side of the harbour to see to your car. It won't hold you up too long then."

"Oh, I'll be in no hurry. This is a glorious spot." He went on to talk of gables and dormers, spindle-banistered staircases, spiral staircases, quoins, which were cornerstones he explained for Dane's benefit. Chloe seemed to know as much as this fellow did. She said, "I'm glad you were still up — it might be you can use it in a book."

Finally Dane yawned pointedly and they took the hint and went to bed.

The mechanic was delayed in coming.

Dane was annoyed, he rather prided himself on making things go. An apprentice was with the mechanic and he drove Clive's car back to the garage. "Too big a job to be done here," Dane told him, "would you like to be shown over the estate, particularly for a view from the top of the headland where you can distinguish quite distinctly the two separate lava flows — one forming our harbour, one Akaroa. Although you'd have to do it on horseback. Do you ride?" The fellow mightn't show to advantage mounted!

Clive agreed readily. "Oh yes, that would be just marvellous although perhaps you are tied up at your desk today? If so, Chloe could take me. When I first came out here, I found out that though she vows she's no expert, Merle's relieving instructor feels she's got a good seat. But we've never been up the headland, only around the shore road."

"I know you need the time at your desk, Dane, so we can easily go alone," Chloe said.

He answered abruptly. "No, I don't like people riding over this terrain unaccompanied. I'll come."

Chloe was conscious of amusement! That would make him realise experimenting wasn't always successful.

Just when the horses were saddled and ready, the extension in the stable rang. Abbie called out. "Phone for you, Dane, better come back to the house."

"Why? I can take it just as well here. Better still ask who and what number and I'll ring back in an hour."

"I'm afraid you can't, dear boy. It's London calling, and it's a person-to-person call. It's Miles. It could be you need to have a manuscript handy, or some other papers, like contracts or something. Thank goodness I caught you. Don't waste any time."

He didn't, but he was left with the picture of Chloe in her riding kit — it was a wonder she'd bothered to change out of those brown slacks, but then she probably knew very well how the putty-coloured jodhpurs suited her — the red hair caught back under her helmet. He'd noticed this morning at breakfast that no bootlace tied it back; a much more feminine bow of golden ribbon adorned it.

"Well, so long, Dane. We'll be back long before the car is brought back. You'd better hurry; publishers *I* would regard like time and tide, waiting for no man." She dug her heels in and her horse took off at a canter; Clive wheeled his mount and was after her.

It was a knotty problem. It took time. When he finally emerged Abbie was in the kitchen concocting a delicious-looking pie from some leftover cooked topside steak. Dane looked at her suspiciously. "I'm sure that guy would have been quite content with a snack. No need for all this."

Abbie trimmed the edges with a fluted fork in quite a design. "I happen to know he's very fond of pastry and I do like cooking for someone who is fond of his food."

Happen to know! Then he must have been a frequent visitor before Dane got back. He walked to the window, looked uphill, said tetchily, "I'd have preferred to be with them. With so little rain lately the ground's as hard as iron and the tussock dry and slippery."

Abbie's tone was casual. "Oh, not to worry. He's no amateur — didn't you realise? He does showjumping. He's kept it up. Not one to be so absorbed in his career that he hasn't time for sport — and other things! And it will do Chloe good — she's been far too immersed in work, especially in our village houses."

When they came back Chloe was sparkling-eyed and had a high colour. "We went as far as Pukemata and were lucky enough to catch Robin — the relief instructor — free. Couldn't have been better. Did your phonecall involve you in much?"

It was purely a polite question. "It did.

One of the lesser enjoyable moments of writing. You think that you've got everything sewn up and a glitch happens and it's one I dare not neglect. Endless looking-up for copyrights in a quotation I've used three times."

"Then you mustn't let me hold you up," offered Clive. "As soon as that mechanic brings back the car I'll be off. I guess you'll need Chloe's help in tracing it. She has told me she doesn't know whether she's an interior decorator or a secretary these days. I can guess which comes to her the more naturally. Still it's lucky for you she's not tied to a deadline." There was an awkward pause.

It was bridged by a thumping sound from upstairs. Chloe exclaimed exasperatedly: "That darned cat! Solomon! My wardrobe door is warped. Natural in older houses, but he loves to nestle in among my longer dresses. I had to get endless gray hairs off my black skirt when Clive took me to Cherrington Lodge for dinner the other night. Jeremy wanted to interview me about interior decorating, from cottages to castles. I find I'm a larger frog in a smaller pool than ever in England. I'll probably put on airs and get cut down to size when I get back."

Another awkward pause. Then Clive filled

it in. "Never mind. Robin wants me to accompany one of her horses to the UK for a special event. Gives me the chance of seeing Chloe in her own environment. Leonora has kindly asked me to stay with them. Can't believe my incredible luck. To see some of those events as they happen instead of just on the screen is unbelievable, and to have Chloe as a bonus, someone in my own line, makes it better still. My partner has a very promising student who qualified last year, quite pleased to gain experience."

Chloe said innocently, oh, much too innocently, "Dane, I expect it will be okay if I take the Toyota and run Clive over to the garage. It *would* save time."

Dane agreed reluctantly. "Best thing to do, it will save my time too. I'll hand her this — she has this incredible memory for quotations, and it will stand me in good stead today, so . . ." His look was full of meaning.

Clive took the hint. "Come on, wench, we're holding this famous author up."

Wench! Dane's pet name for her. And she had told him once that though it was Tudor, she liked it. They departed for Harvest Moon Bay.

Dane found his research fruitless. What a

day to be cooped up here. He *should* be able to concentrate, with the house to himself. Joshua and Abbie were visible through his side window, happily tacking up old-fashioned roses on a trellis at the side. The sound of their shared laughter came to him on the crystal-clear air. Last night had been one of ebony shadows and silver surge, and he'd had to work! Another sound came to him. Blast Solomon! Why couldn't he just snuggle down and snooze? But what if Chloe had slammed the door shut and hadn't realised he was in there? He'd have to go up, haul him out and jamb a chair against it. He took the stairs at a run, found it was indeed shut, tugged and it flew open to reveal not only an offended cat, white whiskers bristling against his striped coat, but two heavy, ancient gilt picture frames. What the devil?

Solomon fled downstairs uttering offended yowls as he went and Dane hauled the pictures out. There it was, Verena's self-portrait, very much as he remembered it from that one disinterested glimpse years ago. Very beautiful, a face schooled to discipline, a hint of sadness about the eyes, an exquisitely curved mouth, and a dented-in chin like Chloe's, *and the tiki*. He'd never told Chloe it was an old family heirloom, given to Gregory Inglethorpe in the long-ago by a Maori friend, in return for saving his child from the waters of the creek after torrential rain. Dane's mother had given it to him. "For the love of your life," she had said whimsically. The *tiki* that had lain against the warmth of Chloe's cleavage. And she'd not known its story or asked one thing about it.

All sorts of thoughts chased through his mind. What were these here for, hidden? And where had she found them? He remembered the nailed-up door, her denial of any revealed treasure. What were they destined for? More pertinent, where were they going to end up? In that New Zealand room of Leonora's? Perhaps Chloe had inherited the antique buyer's love of a bargain. No, not a bargain — it savoured of theft. No wonder she'd been so cool to him ever since he came back. She'd had this in mind. Maybe on her return she'd set wheels in motion re her claim, *and* to a share of the estate! He'd turned up a few new facts while in England, but he'd not been sure till now. Till he'd seen again the portrait, so like Chloe.

He sat on in his study, elbows on his desk, his chin sunk in his hands, uncaring about obscure quotations, or the ebony shadows, or crystal glints of moonlight on the little waves that creamed back from the sand shore — where once they had shared a magic moment, his commitment, and another when he had been fatuous enough to tell her he'd like to see those copper tresses spread out on *his* pillow! What a gullible fool he'd been. Chance of a lifetime, a trip to New Zealand, a good wage, and what fun to be able to find out how profitable the estate was. With mild dalliance as a sideline. But not a sideline on his part.

The clock struck three and he roused himself. He must get the glitch attended to. What had Chloe said, about publishers as well as tides waiting upon no men? He mustn't let Miles down, much as he'd like to saddle Hercules and ride like the wind. He'd have to postpone the showdown till days later. He found the quotation. He wished he'd never used that incident, that he'd never regarded it as of such importance. Meantime, he'd treat her with uncaring politeness, with coolness. But now, he must get on with this — this devilish snag.

His eyes fell on her copy of Palgrave's Treasury which she never travelled without, she had said. He had found endearing, the besotted fool! It was old, tattered. It fell open at the flyleaf, and there it was on a bookplate, in a schoolgirlish hand, her name, Chloe V. Lambard. He knew then without shadow of doubt that the initial would stand for Verena.

Chapter Ten

For the first time ever she found it hard to concentrate on her work. The heart had gone out of it, out of her. It had been a labour of love, but not any more. Outwardly things were the same as before but it was almost torture to be living in the same house feeling as she did. When she wandered the shore she heard no sweet songs now. No wonder Verena had played those lonely unhappy airs on her violin. Chloe wished she herself played some music that could ease this pain. Instead she took to sketching small lovely nooks and crannies of the house and garden. Not paintings. She would do as Verena had done — packed sketches; and then with thirteen thousand miles separating her from Gregory had brought those sketches to life with all the brilliant colours of this country. And had written that poem, possibly with the realisation that she had known another nostalgia but too late, too late.

She noticed a slight change in Dane's attitude towards her. Perhaps he — the great unfeeling hulk — had noticed her coolness, that she sought the company of Abbie and Joshua now more than his. There were hours sandwiched between these swinging moods when she almost drifted into an acceptance of this as natural — you could discipline yourself to anything!

One night they were all in the little sitting-room. A TV programme had just ended. Even as they watched, Dane had been doing some jotting. He said lazily, "Chloe, save me looking up the quotation that's been running like a theme song through my mind all day. I'm too lazy to stir from my chair right now. It begins: 'How do I love thee? Let me count the ways' and for the life of me I can't remember the next line, or who wrote it . . . have you any idea what comes next?"

She hoped none of them heard her swallow or draw the deep breath that was needed to keep her voice matter-of-fact, then said: "It's by Elizabeth Barrett Browning — I do happen to know it. Let me see . . . oh yes. It goes:

'How do I love thee? Let me count the
    ways.
I love thee to the depth and breadth and
    height

My soul can reach . . .'

and the lines I like best are:

> 'I love thee to the level of every
> day's
> Most quiet need, by sun and
> candlelight.' "

She paused and said untruthfully, "I don't recall the rest but at least you'll know where to find it without searching your quotation dictionary."

He said quietly, "I don't need to, except to read the poem to check the punctuation. Those lines are exactly what I need for this incident."

Abbie sighed happily, "I guess you never dreamed, Dane, when you first met Chloe in Leonora's shop, how kindred a spirit she would be — able to quote poetry at the drop of a hat."

Joshua looked sharply at his wife, the look that meant 'Watch it. Don't rush your fences.'

Dane said, "I've a book of hers, a big collection, in the little study."

Chloe knew where. It was off his larger one and as he'd said once: "The study was originally Aubrey and Caroline's bedroom, and the little room off it was for the current baby. True to the pattern of these days it was rarely unoccupied. I keep my holy of holies there. The books that mean most to me, the ones I love to re-read."

Remembrance of that conversation swept across her, undermining the feelings she was fostering about him. So hard not to love him! So she blundered, saying with a slight note of derision, "There's something you might have to watch though. I know you quote poetry in your everyday conversation, often and often, but how many modern heroes do? I suppose it comes naturally to an author. But you might have to be careful. You don't want to be accused by the critics as not being realistic."

Dane looked astonished at this jab from a devout reader, almost as if an inoffensive creature had reared up and bitten him. Then he said dryly, "Perhaps so, if I'd put those words into my hero's mouth, but I'm thinking of someone of Uncle Joshua's age and fluency. I'm getting attached to this man even if he is a figment of my imagination!"

Chloe went bright scarlet, said hastily, "Sorry — I'm abashed. I had no right whatsoever to offer you — bestselling author — cautionary advice."

He said in quite a kindly tone, "Oh not

to worry. Criticism from one who has enjoyed all my books, is quite valuable. It doesn't hurt to have the printed page, even in a thriller, prod some inarticulate husband or lover into a realisation that there is more to relationships than prosaic speech."

Chloe's thoughts flew back to those revealing entries in that notebook and his purpose. She hardened her heart.

Aunt Abbie, still knitting, said complacently, "Well, that's good enough for me. If it hadn't been for Joshua's endearing habit of quoting poetry in his sermons in Edinburgh, and in his everyday speech, I'd never have had the courage to marry him. I felt that there were too many things in which we weren't kindred, you see."

Joshua sat up, "Such as?"

Abbie was unperturbed. "Such as what I considered your inordinate passion for sport, for rugby and cricket. The only sport I was interested in was swimming and then not competitively. I could imagine all our holidays spent climbing heights that gave me vertigo. But then I realised that in marriage there were more hours spent like that line Chloe quoted just now — though I didn't know that poem then — that the candlelight hours spent by one's hearth were what made a marriage. And so it has proved.

And I'm realistic enough to know that some men who aren't articulate by nature, prove their devotion in deeds — caring deeds — rather than words. I'm sure Dane's poetry-loving characters will bear fruit with these strong, silent he-men who can be so boring as husbands. That's why I usually got seated — at the wedding receptions Joshua conducted — beside the father of the bride. I found the romance of the situation seemed to loosen up reticent men and they would start recounting to me, under cover of the buzz of conversation, how they had met and wooed their wives. So I used to advise them to recall those happy hours to their wives and relive some of the romance again."

Joshua started to laugh reminiscently. "And once in between eating and speeches, the chatting suddenly dropped still, and Abbie's voice was heard to proclaim quite loudly, 'I've loved to hear these stories of your own courting days, Mr Ashley, but I do hope you share them with your wife. Joshua and I often do that.' The next moment she realised the lull, and blushed, but the guests, as one, clapped, and later the best man referred to it in his speech as having given him a thrill and he hoped every husband would take heed. It's a memory I treasure," and he indicated with a smile over his open book that it was indeed still treasured.

The atmosphere was very pleasant after that, with Joshua recalling not courting days, but humorous incidents of being a man of the cloth, many of them recalling narrower opinions and incidents of what he called 'the Lord's awkward squad' and then added: "But as a much older minister said to me in my green and salad days, 'If you pride yourself on being tolerant, you must also be tolerant of the intolerant.' It saved me many a time from being too impatient with them."

How Chloe loved them, though there was wistfulness beneath it all. If Dane had been sincere she would love to have lived out the rest of her life in close contact with these dear people. However, as they parted for the night, Dane said, "I could do with a break from my desk, and not spending it trimming sheep-hooves either. How about a good long tramp, Chloe? It's ages since I went right to Camp Bay at the end of the road this side towards the Heads. There's nothing quite like it for the sense of freedom of thought. How about it? We could take sandwiches and fruit, drive past Diamond Harbour and walk from there?"

She managed to keep any hint of desire for just that, out of her tone and said carelessly, "Sorry — but I'm taking the early bus into Christchurch. I want to sketch some quaint old gardens. I think they would make a useful addition to Leonora's New Zealand room."

His tone was just as casual. "Some other time, perhaps."

Chloe's spare time was spent in paying what she supposed would be her last visits to the places she loved here, the dimpled hills, the tiny gullies where the tangy New Zealand bush still existed in all its loveliness like secret glades of Disney-like enchantment.

One day, however, when Joshua and Abbie were in the city and Dane giving a hand with the dipping, she stayed in her room, and after carefully removing the tarnished frame from Verena's portrait, she packed it in tissue paper and carefully stowed it in one of her suitcases. Whether she'd have the courage to actually take it to England she knew not. Probably she wouldn't, but wasn't she entitled to take one souvenir of her time, her joy, her heartbreak, of this lovingly contoured bay away with her? Then, if unable to bear it any longer, or her control snapped, at least it was there ready packed. She carried the frame up to the cubbyhole and pushed it behind that ghastly stack of old-fashioned Venetian blinds, grey-ish-green ones with grubby and rotting tapes. They'd never know that frame hadn't been there when the cupboard was first found. But Verena's portrait really belonged with her other sketches in a place where she was remembered as a loving great-grand-mother, not as one who had deserted her husband, something that led to his death.

There were still moments that she found disarming. Once Dane had come upon Chloe and Sarah unaware. They were both grooming Heloise, and very absorbed. He halted not so much to listen but because if two people were having a serious conversa-tion it was unforgivable to interrupt. Not that Chloe would have put it down to that. She'd probably have thought, once an eaves-dropper, always an eavesdropper! But she did like his comments later.

He heard Chloe say, "I read yesterday in an old paper in the junk-room something I liked very much, Sarah, that I'd like to pass on to you and to Pip. I hope you'll keep the essence of it all your life. It was one of those snippets papers use to fill up short columns. Very simple, the report about a young boy who had such a zest for life that every morning when he woke, he said, 'Good morning, God, good morning world.' I'd like to think you and Pip feel that about each new day. It's infectious, and spreading happiness so important. It reminded me of my grandmother who used to pray for us, my brother and myself, every morning at a quarter to nine when we'd be likely to be starting our day, pray not for good things for us, or for us to do well in our studies and exams, because that was over to us and attention to our homework, but she'd ask that we'd be understanding with less fortunate schoolfellows, that our world would be a better place because we were in it. She told us about this once hoping, I suppose, that knowing what she wished for us would keep us from selfishness, from the hasty and unkind word."

"I like it," admitted Sarah, "I like it very much. You won't forget to tell Pip will you, because I might not get it right. Heloise, do stand still. Pity you aren't thankful like the cats are when they're being brushed — if only you could purr!"

Chloe burst out laughing and gave Sarah a hug. "Oh how priceless. The image *that* conjures up is gorgeous. Your uncle should use it in a book sometime. Have I your permission to tell him? Because even in his thrillers he makes room for humour and does it jolly well."

A voice behind them made them jump. "No need to ask, I heard all that and I'd love to use it."

Sarah's eyes sparkled. "Oh goody!"

Dane then said very deliberately, "And I liked what I heard earlier, too. Thank you for passing that on to my niece. I hope she'll remember it and pass it on to her own children and tell them *who* told *her*."

In spite of the feeling of outrage that still possessed her, moments like these weakened her resolve to confront him with the knowledge that she knew about his cold-blooded planning. It had fitted in well with the necessity for bringing Inglethorpe House back to its former glory. Would she ever come across the situation in a book in years to come? At the thought of years between now and then she felt desolate.

It was that night that Joshua looked across at Dane who was turning over pages of a book as if he were in search of something. He said, "What are you after, Dane, and what book is it?"

"One of I.M. Montgomery's."

"You mean the *Anne of Green Gables* author?"

"Yes. Don't sound so surprised, dear uncle. After all, if Mark Twain and a former British prime minister could write to her to say how they had enjoyed the characters she had created, why should I not be interested? I particularly wanted to re-read a story that one of her characters told. I remember Mother saying she had read the story of her tenacious climb to fame in the teeth of many rejections at first — this was written in 1917 — and she said she had used the story of her own forebear. That somewhere around 1775 the husband, with his family, migrated to Canada and his wife, on arrival, was so homesick she pleaded with him to take them back, and to underline her determination she refused to take her bonnet off till he did. The husband won and they believed she finally settled quite happily. But it proves the point, as in our own family, that homesickness can be truly a sickness of the soul and really be deadly, as Verena's was, breaking two hearts. But today it would be so different, one's own family could visit here, come for special occasions — as long as one was prepared to work hard to provide the wherewithal."

They all sat silently, and the spirit of Verena seemed to invade the air.

Then Abbie said with a sigh, "I'm afraid

you can't turn the clock back, dear boy. But I'm glad you can feel like this for the one who suffered just that, here, lonely in spite of its beauty."

Joshua got up and said briskly, "Well to cheer us all up I'm going to heat these delicious-looking bacon and egg pies to go with our last cuppa. We can't bring back yesterday. It just wasn't in her design for living."

Dane went out to help his uncle. What a complex man he was.

During the small hours of the morning she woke up and decided she'd better be more honest with them all. Oh yes, it mustn't weaken her resolve to go back home, but she would leave the portrait behind, with a note. Perhaps she could pretend she'd wanted to touch it up before telling them she found it. But she was sure she could be convincing about her reasons for going back. She would say her real career lay in the older history and buildings of Great Britain. That this had been a wonderful experience and some day, perhaps in a few years' time, she would pay them a visit to see the restored village, deserted no longer. There were some very good firms in Christchurch only too glad of the work and she would be able to take her dreams back to the familiar and dear places and in time they would stop missing her. Her conscience more at ease, she fell asleep again.

It was some days later. Chloe had made tentative enquiries by phone, not giving her name or number, about timetables and routes home. She wouldn't go the way they had come. That was too full of memories. Their first kiss, snatched in a plane full of other people . . . No, she'd fly to Auckland, thence to Los Angeles, and on to Heathrow. In the last two days Chloe had packed a good many of her things. Not that she was going secretly, but best to be ready as far as she dared. It would put paid to Joshua and Abbie's dream of moving to their loved little house, but they'd probably come around to thinking he was a confirmed bachelor and could make out quite well with a housekeeper. He'd have solitude anyway, in which to write, and in a close community like this, would never be lonely. He'd often be at Phyl's for meals, superb meals at that. But he had enjoyed her Yorkshire pudding with golden syrup. Oh, Chloe Lambard, don't be stupid. He'd have still the kindred companionship of the Reverend Joshua and dear Abbie, and in addition he'd often be with Barry and Monica, and before long,

Roddy and Merle. At which thought, meant to be comforting, tears rolled down her cheeks and splashed the page of the note about the picture, that she had just started. She crumpled it up impatiently, flung it in her wastepaper basket.

She loved this funny little cubbyhole, the sense of being shut away from other distractions in a little tower of her own.

She got up and went to the window and to its magnificent view. It was all there . . . the busy port with its old, restored time-ball; the tall ships; its memories of Captain Robert Falcon Scott and his gallant crew; of Felix von Luckner of the compassionate heart; of those hardy pioneer folk who had travelled so many weary months, sometimes tossed about by storm, sometimes becalmed; the lack of fresh diet; the sudden epidemics, so often among treasured children, who never reached the land of new desire but were consigned to the uncaring deep.

Chloe pulled open a shallow drawer in her worktable, took out a dried-up orange starfish. That, at least, she would take with her. She would leave the *tiki*. She had more than an idea it was the one Verena — dear Greeny of her earliest memories — had worn for her self-portrait, weary hours spent looking at herself in the mirror. Time to be done with sadness. Leonora had said once she was a person who shed kindness and laughter, like sunshine and said how Big Grandad had loved her. Chloe was fiercely glad she had those fragmented memories. That it hadn't been all sadness for that sad girl.

She turned from the window. Have done with these vain regrets. Dane was a charmer, a trifler, so devoted to his work, so, so experimental. Suddenly she was resolved. Tonight she would simply announce that she really must go back to the career she had trained for, that she had already made some enquiries.

Chloe looked down at her paint-stained overall with distaste. Why she even had splashes on her sandals. What was the use of those lovely clothes Gran had bought her for the trip — simply hanging in her wardrobe and rarely worn? Clothes could make you more sure of yourself, give you courage. Dane wasn't about. A lamb buyer had called and he and Ross were up the hill with him. A tui sang sweetly from the flax bush it was perched on — the white feathers at its throat showing against the black curve of the flower stems it had just dipped into. The sweetness of its song seemed as if it was drunken with the honey. She waited for that last note — how had Dane described it? Like wings brushing against a woodland harp . . . one of the songs borne here upon the wind. She shook her mind free, went down one flight and had a shower, paid more attention to her make-up than usual, and tied her hair back, not with a bootlace, but still severely, with a green tartan ribbon Abbie had given her one day.

She slipped into a green frock that had a shimmer of a silver thread in it somewhere. Dane had liked her in it. Oh damn Dane — he obtruded into her thoughts all the time. She'd wear the *tiki,* perhaps for the last time. She put the hanger back and saw Verena's portrait, or at least the back of it. She didn't allow herself to turn it round.

Abbie was calling from below. "Chloe, I'm off to join Joshua at our house. I'm taking a picnic lunch over. Would you give Dane his lunch if he doesn't stay for it at Phyl's? But if he brings that buyer over, you could grill some chops and tomatoes for them."

"Will do," replied Chloe. Suddenly she knew what she'd do with the picture. She'd take it down and put it in a cupboard in the little room off his main study, where he kept the books best-loved and often re-read.

She'd put it right at the back of the stores of paper always kept there.

She lingered, wandering around, picking out a book here and there at random. She smiled at some of the inscriptions, some written in an immature schoolboy hand. There was one, a book of Walter de la Mare's and the flyleaf said, 'Bought this with money I actually earned by my pen. An Auckland newspaper. It's a start.' Another was marked, 'To our son, congratulations, to celebrate your success in coming first in New Zealand with that article on old Akaroa. Love Mum and Dad.'

Chloe's eyes misted over. She would have liked to have known them.

She heard voices. Oh bother, Dane must be bringing in the buyer. She must think up some excuse for being in here, in his inner room. But she didn't need an excuse. They stopped in the big study and that wasn't the buyer — it was a woman's voice. There seemed to be strong emotion in it. It said, "Oh Dane, Dane, what a mess I've made of things."

Then Dane's voice: "It will come out all right, darling. It's got to. Now hush, there, there!" That meant she was in his arms, he would be patting her back, and holding her close.

"Don't be too upset, Elise, just pull yourself together. I'll make you some coffee, seeing you're determined not to stay. But you must have something before you set off back to Akaroa. And take all care on the road. I'm sorry things got out of hand. We need some time to ourselves. But this Chloe girl is around somewhere."

Chloe burned with indignation. *This Chloe girl!* Like a wretched nuisance. And why, why? It sounded clandestine. That was confirmed almost immediately. Dane said, "I know what I'll do. I'll come over next week on some pretext or other. After all I've got a very fertile imagination. I'll think of something. But give me a ring, on the quiet, to make sure Ken's out. Now come into the kitchen. We'll have a snack there. Chloe appears to be out. Probably wandering along the bay. She won't think anything if she comes in."

Chloe was left in the little study, and knew this just confirmed her distrust. She dared not emerge — and turn up in the kitchen. Those creaking boards would give her away. Barry was to fix them when he had time. And she was starving. She hadn't bothered with morning tea. She sat down and tried to interest herself in a book. Mercifully they didn't take long. She heard the car, presumably this Elise's, take off. No doubt some fascinating French woman, or at least of French descent, seeing she came from Akaroa, over the hill, where they had hoped to take over New Zealand for the French!

She heard the last farewells murmured, then Dane's footsteps. Oh, horrors, he was coming back here. There was nothing she could do. Would he settle down at his desk and not come in here? She was trapped. Suddenly, faced with this confirmation of his perfidy, it was too much for her and next moment Dane was faced with a termagant in green, eyes flashing, bosom heaving, cheeks flying flags of real rage.

"So!" she said. "So, you're revealed in your true colours at last! And this time it's not for the sake of some future novel, not an experiment — a cold-blooded experiment with a woman's emotions — with a girl as green as I was! But not any more! The sooner I'm out of this bay the better."

Dane gazed at her. "I haven't the faintest idea what you're talking about. And Elise —"

"I don't want to hear about Elise, about your shoddy little affair. I'm sorry for this Ken whoever he is. I'd seen through you long since, you and your insincerity. The way you use flattering words as the tools of your trade, just so you can see a girl's re-action to thinking herself the object of your devotion."

Suddenly Dane came to life. "Reaction? But that's what you are — the object of my devotion, though you've changed so since I got back. Aunt Abbie's been hinting you find my absorption in my work too much but I don't think it's that, you seemed to understand it so well at first. I believe you've fallen for Clive Douglasson — why he had to turn up I don't know. I suppose you're infatuated with the thought that he's in the same line as you but —"

Chloe scoffed. "Clive Douglasson noth-ing! He's head over heels in love with Robin at the stables. It *is* just a case of being interested in the same line of work — what I'm mad about is your experimentation."

A light flashed into the tawny eyes. He said, "Ah, now we're getting somewhere! What experimentation?" He stepped for-ward and caught her by the upper arms in a grip that hurt.

"As if you didn't know!"

"But I don't — I —" He got no further. She had whipped across to one of the drawers. "You'll know in a moment — it's here, all down in black and white. What you wrote in that restaurant in Seddon Halt that day after sneakily eavesdropping, and made up your mind that there was the love interest Miles wanted deepened. And you even added to it the same night. Oh, how I despise you — using your liking for poetry and *my* liking for it to take me in — and I had the bonus of being trained in re-decorating and none of it meant a thing, more fool I! But —"

"Now shut up — and I mean, shut up. I can see how damning that was, written on the spur of the moment — not realising I was about to meet you — you were only a voice at the other side of that partition. Oh girl can't you realise what it meant to me — you said you didn't believe in love at first sight; well neither do I, but I do believe in love at first hearing, now! Which is a darned sight more reliable than books.

"I thought to myself, here's a girl of spirit, fond of Shakespeare's sonnets, expecting a proper wooing — oh, I could have clapped as you flashed by, like a comet streaking across the sky; a moment seen, then gone forever. It did something to me. I thought it was meant to be when I met you half an hour or so later! And I thought you were meeting me halfway — till you started rebuffing me at every turn; it got me on the raw at times, made me feel frustrated. Yet there were tender moments. For a girl who didn't want a prosaic proposal you're the limit. If you *can't* care for me I'll have to take it. But if that's so I made a perfect fool of myself when I took that recent trip to England. I could shake you till your teeth rattle. How could you? I did indeed spread my dreams under your feet and you didn't tread softly. You walked over them in hob-nailed boots! Why even when I found out who you were — discovered Verena's portrait hidden in your wardrobe — I went on loving you. I'd suspected for some time, felt sore with Leonora that she'd sent you to spy out the land as it were, but then I love you too, love your whole family. What —"

"Yes, what?" she said, and suddenly she lost all her bright colour. "What are you going to do about Elise? I eavesdropped too, you see!"

The next moment her fury rose again, for unforgivably he laughed. "What am I going to do? I'm going to sort out this stupid financial bother she's got herself into that she can't be persuaded she ought to make a clean breast of to her husband — I've lent her the money to put it right. Chloe — Elise is my cousin and I'm very fond of her. But she's a featherhead." He stopped and something flashed into his eyes, narrowing them.

"Why, I believe this meant you were jealous and that means you *do* care. Girl, don't you realise you are the very core of my being, that I dreaded the thought of homesickness for you — kept talking about a shrinking world, of quite frequent visits you could pay home, of the visits your people could pay here? In fact they are coming! Leonora came up trumps bless her and says she knows someone who can look after the shop for them for a month. And we'll get this business sorted out once and for all. I could still choke you for letting me go on searching those old records, but we'll get it all sorted out. Your inheritance will give you means of your own. We'll —"

She was staring at him. "Inheritance — what do you mean? What —"

"Gregory's will — you're the descendant he so desired to benefit. Oh Chloe, Chloe, I love you — *love you* — tell me you love me too. What are you looking like that for?"

"I'm not the descendant of Verena and Gregory. How could you think that? You haven't said anything to Gran or Mum and Dad? No you couldn't have or they'd have put you right. How dare you think that I came here for financial reasons? Greeny was only my great-grandmother in the bonds of love — and all she did for Leonora, a poor bewildered child whose parents were taken from her in one fell swoop. Oh, she should have told you she wanted me to come out to see where her loved foster mother had once lived and painted and made the mistake of her life when she left this glorious spot. Only I think so many cruel things were said to her because of Gregory dying like that, that Gran never dwelt on it. Verena not only lost her husband, Dane, she lost her baby, a son, prematurely, stillborn. But she made up for her foolishness in the way she gave my grandmother a home, and love, all the love there was." She stopped, said uncertainly, "Dane?" and there could be no doubt to the man in front of her, at the love-light in those sea-green eyes.

He took a step forward, caught her hands, said: "Oh girl . . . that day at the water's edge, didn't I say it was a commitment? As it was — forever. I'm waiting for you to say the words I want to hear — Chloe, my darling, don't hold out on me."

She burst out, "Oh Dane — I love you, of course I love you. I've been so unhappy."

He gave an exultant laugh, caught her close and sighed. "I hope it's the last time you'll ever be unhappy because of me."

He looked deep into her eyes, then she was enfolded in a heart-hungry embrace, and his mouth reached for hers.

When he finally lifted it he said, "Oh the wonderful moments ahead of us and think of the joy it will bring everyone — your father will be wondering what has taken me so long; nothing prosaic about *my* wooing, my love — I practically reverted to the Victorians and asked him for your hand! And just think of the joy it is going to give Joshua and Abbie to say nothing of my grandparents — my true reason for taking you to Wheatacres was so they could meet you, and Gran whispered to me, 'So this will be the girl of your heart who must have the *tiki*.'"

They heard voices and looked along that little path made of the stones of the hills, embedded in the earth, and saw Joshua and Abbie, he with secateurs, Abbie with a trowel in her hand ready to get some treasure of the old garden for the new.

"Let's go and tell them how near their dream is," said Dane. "It cuts short this incomparable hour, but there will be other hours. Many of them."

There were, with the sweetest hour of all later that night when darkness fell and Dane took her up the little stairway to the admiral's quarterdeck.

They stood there, hand in hand, the embroidered cloth of heaven above them. "I feel as if the very stars are listening and are glad," Dane whispered, then added, "I think Verena would be glad too that Leonora's granddaughter came here and loved the scenes she realised too late she had loved too. And she'd be glad that you didn't have to suffer a divided heart like she did. That you can have the best of both worlds, the old and the new."

Chloe said softly, "But I know which world is the dearest to *me*. It's wherever *you* are, Dane." She continued dreamily, "There's magic in the web of it," and they both laughed and said together "Shakespeare!"

Dane said, "God bless William."

Chloe felt the stars shone brighter in salute.

Dane's voice was a little shaky and it was just light enough for her to see those tell-tale lines about his mouth. "It's for another poet to set the seal on the rest of our lives — listen: 'How do I love thee? Let me count the ways . . .' " and he gathered her close.